The SLATE of LIFE

The SLATE of LIFE

More Contemporary Stories by Women Writers of India

Edited by Kali for Women

Introduction by Chandra Talpade Mohanty and Satya P. Mohanty

The Feminist Press
at The City University of New York
New York

Published 1994 by The Feminist Press at The City University of New York
311 East 94 Street, New York, NY 10128

94 95 96 97 98 5 4 3 2 1

"Grandmother's Letters" appeared originally in *House of a Thousand Doors* by Meena Alexander (Washington, D.C: Three Continents Press, 1988).

"The Offspring" by Indira Goswami appeared originally in *Indian Literature* 112 (New Delhi: Sahitya Akademi, 1986).

Library of Congress Cataloging-in-Publication Data

The Slate of life : more contemporary stories by women
writers of India / edited by Kali for women ; introduction by
Chandra Talpade Mohanty and Satya P. Mohanty.
p. cm.
Originally published: New Delhi: Kali for Women, 1990.
ISBN 1-55861-087-1 : $35.00. — ISBN 1-55861-088-X (pbk.) : 12.95
1. Short stories, Indic—Women authors—Translations into English.
2. Short stories, English—Women authors—Translations from Indic languages.
I. Kali for Women (Organization)
PK5461.S52 1994
891'.1—dc20 94-32543
CIP

This publication is made possible, in part, by public funds from the National Endowment for the Arts and the New York State Council on the Arts. The Feminist Press is also grateful to Joanne Markell and Genevieve Vaughan for their generosity.

Cover art: *Celebrate the Joy of Reading*
© 1994 by Manjula Padmanabhan
Cover and text design: Paula Martinac
Typeset by Mod Komp Corp.
Printed in the United States of America on acid-free paper
by McNaughton & Gunn, Inc.

Contents

Preface

Ten years ago when Kali for Women launched our series of stories by women, published in translation from various Indian languages, there were few precedents or guideposts that we could follow. English translations existed, in some sufficiency—novels by well-known writers; occasional anthologies of stories, some that uncovered new talent; and regular attempts by various regional academies of literature to present award-winning and good new writing in English. Special issues of journals, at least one devoted entirely to variety in translation, also appeared from time to time.

But ours was a somewhat different endeavor, part of a project to identify and publish women's writing as a whole, a distinct genre. A writing that is as much creative as it is a considered and unique commentary on the world the writers inhabit, the society they observe and then hold up for inspection, the mores they challenge. A writing that is "political" even while it may be intensely personal; a writing that, in patriarchal societies, is potentially subversive.

Our other objective was to try and make available as wide a range of creative writing as possible from the different regions and literatures in India so that, over time, we would have not only diversity, but, we hoped, a reasonably representative collection of writing by women from 1900 onward.

It has not been easy, but it has always been thrilling. In the beginning it was difficult to find good translators, to find them in as many as ten different languages for a single anthology, to insure fidelity to the original and fluency in English in all ten, to retain the regional flavor while presenting an Indian oeuvre. But what a veritable treasure of writing was excavated once we tapped the vein. *Truth Tales,** our first anthology, published in 1986, has stories from eight languages; *The Slate of Life* has stories from ten; and both have been further translated into French, German, and Spanish.

*U.S. edition published by The Feminist Press in 1990.

A novella about a child-widow, written originally in Kannada, was published in English by us in 1990 and is now available in Japanese.

We are often asked by our readers how we select material for translation. In a country the size of India this process—of locating writers in the indigenous languages—almost has to be a random one. How do you choose? How *can* you choose? If we were to attempt to be systematic, we could perhaps start from the southern tip of the country and work our way northward and westward and eastward. But then the enterprise would take several generations. Instead, over time, we have developed our own, rather random, methods. We publish collections of stories from different languages; we locate these by scouring journals and magazines, and by relying on friends and supporters.

In the years since we began this work, women's writing has become more visible, more recognized, and, we believe, much more widely read. The practice of translation itself, particularly of writing by women, has inspired serious reflection, and many universities have initiated research on this subject through their women's studies centers. Because autobiographical, fictional, "personal" writing has traditionally been more accessible to women, it is these genres that are now being translated and published, more and more.

Publishing books like *The Slate of Life* is only part of our total publishing activity at Kali. Our commitment is to women's writing and writing on women, as a whole. But the excitement of discovering a new, unknown, untranslated woman writer from one of our languages is something that we have found hard to match.

Urvashi Butalia and Ritu Menon
Kali for Women

Chandra Talpade Mohanty and
Satya P. Mohanty

Lives of Their Own

As in the North American, European, and African contexts, it is primarily in the last twenty years that feminists in India have begun to retrieve and interpret women's literature in a systematic way. The Indian literary canon remains male dominated, and the publication and dissemination of women's texts should be viewed in the context of the rise of the 1970s feminist movement. This collection of short stories translated from nine Indian languages is in part the product of a new cultural and political environment in which traditional masculinist visions of nationhood and social justice are being revised.[1]

With the exception of Indira Goswami and Meena Alexander, all of the writers in *The Slate of Life* were born in the 1920s and 1930s and came of age in the midst of the anticolonial struggle. All but Saraswathi Amma (the first self-proclaimed feminist in Malayalam literature) and Dhiruben Patel began publishing their work after Indian independence in 1947, at a time when all efforts were directed to the making of the nation and, by implication, the making of a national literature. This historical background helps us understand why the writers in *Slate* have chosen to write about the subjects they write about, and perhaps even the ideological and stylistic choices they make in their writing.[2] These ten stories provide evidence of women writing themselves into history. Recording and analyzing gender identities, challenging sexual exploitation and brutality as well as the less obvious forms of symbolic and cultural power, they urge the reader to reimagine family, community, and nation.

The form of the short story is significant in this context because it is conducive to publication in magazines and journals, which have large circulations in the regional languages. The choice of the short story may also be gender-specific—it can be written in a shorter amount of time, time often snatched away from the everyday work of domestic and social responsibilities. It is a form that often best records the vicissitudes of familial, domestic, and sexual arrangements which women writers explore in great detail. The short story thus provides glimpses into everyday life, the "slate of life," and can reach popular audiences. Moreover, it allows a number of stylistic choices, from psychological and social realism to fantasy and traditional forms of storytelling. There is perhaps a relationship between the short story and oral narratives, which have always been a significant form of literary and cultural expression in India, since they serve to record popular memory and history. At least one of the stories in *Slate*—"Lata" by Binapani Mohanty—explicitly invokes the orality of Indian literary traditions.

The collection includes translations from nine Indian languages: Urdu, Oriya, Hindi, Malayalam, Punjabi, Tamil, Assamese, Gujarati, and Bengali. The first story, by Meena Alexander, is the only one originally written in English. Generally speaking, except for English and Hindi, the different languages belong to particular regional states or provinces, each with its own culture (or subculture within the national culture). For instance, Assamese is spoken in Assam, Oriya in Orissa, and Gujarati in Gujarat. Thus, while translations of these stories into English makes a national readership possible, originally most of the stories were written for and read by more local geographical and linguistic communities.[3]

The Slate of Life is an ideal text for use in the classroom at a time when questions of diversity and pluralism are at the center of feminist activism and scholarship. In the following introduction to the stories we provide a brief account of each, with an explanation of the way experiences and identities are fundamentally *gendered*. An attempt to understand the gendered aspect of our lives is part of a larger process by which women (and men) reimagine and remake their social worlds. Our primary focus is thus on the moral and political agency of the women characters, rather than on their status as mere victims or objects of patriarchal domination. Our theoretical assumption—one we share with many feminist scholars—is that an account of the latter is incomplete and inadequate without an understanding of the former.[4]

Gender, Experience, Identity

The stories in *Slate* may be approached in terms of the following question: In what ways do women come to terms with the social fact of gender, that is, the socially determined relationships of hierarchy and inequality that govern their experiences and shape the choices and possibilities that are available to them? This is one of the central theoretical questions of all feminist inquiry, and writings by and about women offer a special place where its implications can be explored. The question breaks down into two related concerns: (1) how do girls and women acknowledge, understand, and come to terms with the gendered identities they inherit? and (2) how do they imagine and subsequently live the new alternative identities they construct? In both situations, gender is part of a larger web of social entanglements, of complexly interwoven meanings and values that are tied to class, race, caste, age, religion, or region.

While "gender" seems to be an abstract or theoretical notion, its importance becomes obvious once we begin to reflect on our daily lives. It profoundly affects (and is in some ways shaped by) our everyday experiences as social beings. Gender is *causally* relevant to our lives, to the choices that are available to us, and that is why—as feminists have always pointed out—our personal experiences need to be seen as socially and politically significant. Experience might not be a self-evident source of knowledge but, when interpreted correctly, it can give us valuable information about key features of our social world. Our experiences have a cognitive component; they can yield insights about our social and cultural identities, both those we inherit and those we wish to remake in the light of our moral and political commitments. There is a continuity between experience and identity, and literary works are often the best places to perceive this. They help us see how (gendered) experiences and identities are not merely the personal views or perspectives of an individual, but rather the spaces where political meanings are articulated, spaces where an accurate knowledge of our social world can be sought.[5]

All of the stories in *Slate* raise questions of gender identity—of location, agency, and the reimagining of the social. In culturally specific ways, each story engages questions of sexual politics (the regulation, control, and use of sexuality) as it explores the conditions and moments of resistance to dominant patriarchal paradigms. We will discuss the stories in three groups, each organized around a cluster of related themes or issues.

Sexuality and Subjectivity

Chudamani Raghavan's "Counting the Flowers," Dhiruben Patel's "Crushed Flowers," Wajida Tabassum's "Hand-Me-Downs," and Binapani Mohanty's "Lata" constitute the first set of stories. While they write in different languages (Gujarati, Tamil, Urdu, and Oriya, respectively), these women are contemporaries who produced much of their work in the mid 1950s through 1970s, in the context of the building of a newly independent nation, amid debates about the modernization of India, the transformation of traditional patriarchies, and the role of women as the cultural and moral arbiters of family and community values. This context helps explain the immediate significance of their feminist vision: all four stories explicate in great detail the latent violence directed against women in the routines and practices of everyday life within the family and the larger community. In each narrative the families and communities, which are supposed to protect and nurture the young women protagonists, are exposed as colluding in controlling and regulating the sexually vulnerable status of the women. The stories provide a way of recognizing and analyzing the significance of experience in the construction of sexual self and agency. We focus here on the tension between inherited gender roles and the search for and refashioning of identities that question patriarchal or masculinist practices and traditions.

Chudamani Raghavan's Tamil story "Counting the Flowers" provides an electrifying account of an ordinary, everyday event: a marriage interview. Much of the power of the story comes from the fact that, while it focuses on the contrast between the ostensible politeness of the encounter and the financial haggling and power struggle that underlie the conversation among the prospective in-laws, the reader's attention is never allowed to drift from Brinda, the bride-to-be. She is the one who is on display, whose value and worth as an individual are soon to be determined within the brutally impersonal terms of social (in particular, sexual and economic) exchange. Brinda's financially strapped parents, well aware of the significance of this possible exchange with a family that is economically much better off, collude in the bartering of their daughter. The father's tone of voice invites the guests to "take a good look" at Brinda (79), and the not-too-subtle looking and being looked at shape the deepest tension and struggle in the story. For while she is admittedly a "wheat-colored vision," with a "luminous air of easy, natural grace" (79) that threatens to overcome the disadvantage of poverty (as easily as "one might shake off a fly" [79]), she is also a commodity to be purchased at the most advantageous price.

> "Please drink your coffee," the girl's father urged, doing the honors.
>
> "Oh yes!" The boy's mother turned to the girl, "How far have you been educated?"
>
> The girl's father gave a start. Had the marriage broker not apprised the bridegroom's party of these details?
>
> "We had to stop her schooling with the Eighth Standard."
>
> "Not good at studies, I suppose?" (79)

Brinda's refusal to participate in this haggling takes the form of looking as well, but it is a looking that introduces (and gradually establishes) a new space, a new and more complex register of valuing and being valued. The nagalinga tree outside the window—with its flowers that combine the twin religious motifs of the lingam (the sacred phallus, emblem of Lord Shiva and of the power and divinity of elemental sexual energy) and the serpent that protects it—is transformed by Brinda's consciousness into a veritable text to be read and reread, an alternative source of personal meaning.

The nagalinga flower has a "beauty all of [its] own" (79), in contrast perhaps to Brinda's immediate situation which makes it impossible for her to claim even her own "luminous air" or her "natural grace." The flowers suggest to her both abundant (sexual) creativity and freedom, "[a] wealth of delicately hued blossoms, silken in their softness" (80). The nagalinga tree is endlessly procreative; it sheds its brown leaves often, and they "pile up [so] thick and high on the ground" that humans have "a tough time sweeping [them] out" (81). "And then," as she tells her parents and her prospective in-laws, blissfully defiant of their expectations of conventional social behavior, "in just a few days, right in front of your eyes, the green leaves appear again, fast and fresh, and cover the entire tree in no time! . . . Even as the dead leaves are falling off, the tiny new green ones are sprouting alongside—what an enchanting sight!" (81). If Brinda's sexuality and, in effect, her very personhood are not her own, it is of course no surprise that by the end of the story the image of the nagalinga tree threatens to exceed its original frame, registering—with its evocation of a violent dismemberment—the pain and the indignity Brinda has been refusing to accept as her own.

The modulation of the image with which Chudamani Raghavan concludes her story may accurately reflect the fears and apprehensions of Dhiruben Patel's narrator about her seventeen-year-old heroine Kushi. Unlike her younger sister, Vaishali, who "suspects the whole world" (102), and her mother who "couldn't forget that [Kushi] is [after all] a girl" (101) in a predatory male world where her sexuality makes her eminently vulnerable, Kaushambi dreams of a utopian life of free sharing and giving, a life where money has no significance and the values of economic exchange have not yet come to govern social relationships.

As the story opens, she flees from her mother's rebuke to a free corner of a narrow corridor, a personal corner from where she can participate in the unselfconscious abundance of their neighbor's garden: "It was a beautiful garden, always green, luxuriating in its solitary happiness. The gardener, too, always looked happy . . . could it be because of the garden?" (100). But when Kushi wishes to be simply "seventeen years old, completely unselfconscious, smiling and talking to anybody who comes along" (101), she cannot, for—as she is reminded ever so often—she is a girl who cannot afford to "indulge in such antics" (100). When the gardener comes close to her, smiles at her, and extends his hand, Kushi is unable to see it as anything but an innocent gesture of affection. She sees herself as existing outside the limiting and limited economic terms of her real social world: "She showered smiles like the parijat tree that showers flowers *for no reason*" (101, emphasis added).

Much like Chudamani Raghavan's Brinda, Dhiruben Patel's young protagonist draws sustenance from a metaphysical view that is deeper than what her immediate social world provides for. Kushi realizes that the flowers she showers on others "would be trod upon or muddied"; but to deal with this reality she points to a natural world beyond the space of scarcity and fear her mother invokes: "other [flowers] will fall still," Kushi thinks, "equally beautiful, delicate, totally pure . . ." (101). While the reader needs to keep in balance the perspectives of Kushi and her mother, it is difficult to ignore the fact that Kushi's view of sexuality as free exchange is a bit too Edenic, for it is itself predicated on an existential attitude of pure defiance. "Old age, sickness, or poverty," she thinks, are part of human life; they can befall "anybody, any time." That is what Kushi fears. "That is why she wants to laugh while she can. She doesn't mind whether it is the postman, the gardener, or the milkman standing before her. She doesn't care about the faces. She just looks at the eyes, full of warmth, full of life. She cannot help responding to the sunrise in their eyes. Let Mother worry about her. Let Vishu prepare a bed of arrows with her piercing questions. She can lie down on it, but as long as her roots are alive she will not perish, will not turn to stone" (103).

Kushi, like Brinda, wants to choose, to be able to fashion her own identity. In the world in which she lives, however, her choices are constrained by the social fact of gender. She is a girl, and that limits her possibilities in ways that are drastic. As she realizes early on in the story she cannot be a "gardener, or a tongawalla, or even a cobbler . . . [she] can't even dream of . . . many interesting careers" (100). She cannot choose to fashion her own sexuality either, to imagine it in utopian terms of abundance and honest sharing. She must learn to read signs, her mother tells her, so that she can distinguish among the various gestures of giving and sharing—the doctor who is happy to delay sending the bill, the gardener who reaches out to touch her hand, the young neighbor who wants her to wear his beautiful wristwatch and bursts into tears when she returns it to him. It is not their sexuality that both Brinda and Kushi must come to acknowledge, these stories remind us, but rather the dimension of their sexuality—and consequently their *selves*—that is necessarily determined by the unequal economic and political relations of a gendered world. The birth of this social consciousness is the focus of both writers, a birth both painful and necessary.

In the case of Brinda and Kushi, the birth of this consciousness is recorded primarily on the symbolic level. In the stories by Wajida Tabassum (originally written in Urdu) and Binapani Mohanty (written in Oriya), however, the drama culminates in an action that is explicitly defiant, transformative, and suggestive of new possibilities. Wajida Tabassum's Chamki is the daughter of a live-in servant woman, a wet nurse working for a rich household. Chamki (literally "one who sparkles or glitters") lives in the shadow of her mistress-friend Shehzadi Pasha, "whose veins," the narrator tells us early in the story, "coursed with the wish to command" (37). Chamki's deprivations are less material than personal; while she has enough clothes to wear, for instance, she can hardly call anything her own. And even the seven-year-old's imagination, which dreams of playing roles and playing with her received social identity, is taught that there are limits.

> Chamki spoke quickly, "Pasha! I was thinking that if you and I exchange our clothes and become odhni badal sisters, then I could also wear your clothes, no?"
>
> "My clothes? You mean all those clothes that are lying in my trunks?"
>
> Chamki nodded uncertainly. Shehzadi Pasha was doubled up with laughter, "Ao, what a foolish girl. You know you are a servant—you wear my discarded things. And all your life you'll wear my hand-me-downs."
>
> Then, with infinite love which held more arrogance than any other feeling, Shehzadi Pasha tossed the dress that she had shed for the bath toward Chamki. "Here, wear this. I have any number of other clothes." (37–8)

Chamki's negotiation with her own subordinate status is an everyday affair. What makes her unique in the story is the fact that she does not reconcile herself to this unfair and unequal social condition. Her questions remain pointed, throwing into stark relief those features of her social and moral world that her mother was chosen to accept: "As she stood there, the little seven-year-old thought deeply and said haltingly, 'Ammavi, if Shehzadi Pasha and I are the same age then why didn't she wear what I took off?'" (38). To a child, age is the only rational determinant of status and authority. When her eminently sensible question is rudely dismissed, Chamki's perspective turns outward to other features of her world, drawing on other criteria of social evaluation: "Ammavi, I'm much prettier than bi Pasha, aren't I? *You* make her wear the clothes I discard'" (39).

While Chamki's questions might seem naive, they in fact embody a moral imperative, based as they are on a view of personal dignity and worth that refuses to endorse the way things are for herself and her mother. Her challenge to her mother is far from childish: "Ammavi, it is one thing to take such gifts because we have little choice, but please don't feel so happy when you take them'" (39). Like Brinda, Kushi, and many of the female protagonists of the stories in this volume, Chamki raises questions about the meaning and implications of what a woman can call her own. If material privation makes her personal situation precariously dependent on those who have more, she is nonetheless eager to value the realm of her freedom, to mark the space where she is in fact free to choose.

Thus when she is given an orange dress of "ordinary material" by the senior Pasha to mark the event of her first recital of the Koran, she treasures it, perhaps because it represents a recognition of what is clearly an achievement. It is something that is her own because it is the product of her personal effort, her "intelligence and [her] interest" in the project (39). And it is the orange dress, the external sign of this personal achievement, that Chamki uses to take her revenge in the end. By then, what is defined as most significant is that social ownership itself become an unstable category, that the rich mistress be shown that money does not determine all the terms of possession and exchange. Chamki is able to do this, tragically enough, by self-consciously reconstructing parts of herself in new ways. Her naturally smiling face becomes a weapon that can be used as a purely political tool. Chamki finally manages to achieve a new kind of exchange with Shehzadi Pasha, but in this exchange the many meanings of ownership are not revised and rewritten but rather exploded, the labor that sought to produce the revisioning anulled. The young servant-girl's "manic laughter" (42) transcends the ideological frame of her mother's subordination in a benevolent but repressive relationship, but it may have nowhere else to go. In the wings, her husband is waiting, the "suitable groom" found by the mistress of the household, the senior Pasha, "a woman of great . . . compassion [who] always considered the welfare of her servants as she did of her own children" (40).

"Counting the Flowers," "Crushed Flowers," and "Hand-Me-Downs" are all set in urban or semi-urban contexts, and their focus is on a segment of the larger society. Binapani Mohanty's Oriya story "Lata" takes us to rural Orissa, where an entire village provides simultaneously the social and moral contexts within which the actions of the protagonist are defined. Binapani Mohanty's interest is less in psychological realism than in outlining in larger-than-life terms the moral implications of her particular story; indeed, this is the one story in the collection that deliberately draws on the generic traditions of the orally transmitted tale. The modulations of voice in "Lata" suggest that its narrator is in fact a member of the village community, perhaps a village elder, (re)telling a story to the young. There is not only a story to be told but also a history to be retrieved and acknowledged. There is an implied contrast between the callousness of the community *then* and its implications for us *now*: "All of them burst into laughter and the wanton breeze wafted it away, who knows where. Still, Lata continued to lie flat on her back, staring blankly at the moon. The festivities of the village remained outside her, did not touch her at all. And no one needed to know the inner world she dwelt in, or where her thoughts lay, save herself" (43). Similarly, a few lines later: "Around midnight . . . Lata shut her front door and left, as though for the Holi festivities. And nobody came near her house, nor cared to inquire where she was" (44). We are reminded in moments like these that part of the act of traditional storytelling consists of stitching together the community through a reactivation of memories and an introduction of new values. Binapani Mohanty's narrator is represented as speaking directly to his or her own community, and the rhetorical questions ("For wouldn't he be mad?" [44]; "But did that happen?" [45]; "But could Jagu get angry with her?" [45]) don't simply depict the informal conversational rhythms of rural Oriya, they also establish the common emotional ground on which the story's deeper moral challenge can be placed.

Lata is the daughter of a poor, low-caste man, Jagu Behera, and her poverty and social marginality shape the central action of the story. After she returns to her father's house, her initial silence about why she left her husband and her in-laws is the silence of a dutiful daughter: she does not want to disrupt the appearance of harmony and normalcy. And it is this appearance that the rich descriptions of the communal festival, Holi, offer the reader as well: "It was the full moon night of Holi, with moonlight splashing over the entire village. The deities had finally been brought to the festival grounds after being carried from house to house. Revellers thronged the narrow village lanes. The children had rested a little in the evening and, refreshed, had gone off to the grounds in a spirit of joy. With hidden handfuls of colored powder they had smeared one another's faces" (43).

But this evocation of communal participation, of harmony and balance (the deities go to everyone's house, for instance), is partial and potentially quite misleading. Against it is outlined Lata's situation, her yet-to-be-named fears that have "settled in like ghosts" (43). The contrast between the appearance of harmony in the community and the reality of sexual violence and exploitation is made clearer later when Lata, having left the village to give birth to her illegitimate child, returns to reclaim her space in the village community.

In reclaiming this space, Binapani Mohanty's heroine in effect reconfigures the ideological space that defines the village community. This is why Lata's rebellion is best read not in realistic or psychological terms alone but primarily through the almost archetypal imagery of the concluding pages. She is not merely claiming that her fatherless child, the product of a communal rape, be recognized as legitimate; her moral and political stance is more brazen, more audacious: the bastard-child will establish a new mode of belonging, a redefined sense of not only self but also his (and her) world.

> She cuddled [the child] close and mumbled, "Why do you cry, my child? Ah, my pet, I am here with you. Don't you worry. Who's there man enough in the world to admit he's your father? There, there, your mother will take care of you."
>
> What the boy understood only he knew, for he flew up into the clouds. He stretched his arms toward the moon and broke into spontaneous laughter. Its sound startled the bystanders, and they started to disperse slowly, their heads lowered . . .
>
> Lata looked around her and spat on the child's tiny chest to ward off the evil eye. . . . She would take care of him. She owned the plot of land that had been her father's, and her son would be its master one day! (49)

Here is a definition of ownership and agency that challenges the symbolic order of the traditional community, and that is presented in stylized form as a composite image. Lata's outburst shames the rapists as well as those who are ideologically complicitous with them. She stands "stern and full of purpose" (48) while "the old woman . . . flop[s] down on the veranda, as though spent. Ramu, Bira, Gopi, Maguni and Naria [keep] their eyes on the ground" (48–9). The makers of the old community "disperse slowly, their heads lowered"; in more ways than the obvious ones, they "hobbled away in silence" (49). The humble one-room hut of the low-caste Jagu Behera becomes the site of a transfer of symbolic power. Instead of the traditional festival grounds where the story opens, we see at the end how the center of moral gravity shifts to this hitherto "abandoned" space, with the daughter claiming both ownership and the right to create new meaning for herself, her son, and her community.

"Lata" completes a cycle that we have been tracing through the stories by Chudamani Raghavan, Dhiruben Patel, and Wajida Tabassum.

The sexuality of the young women protagonists leaves them vulnerable to exploitation and violence, but it can also constitute the space where a certain political interrogation and knowledge are possible. This knowledge is of both limits and possibilities; it outlines the realm of inherited social identities and of new and alternative visions, simultaneously personal and political.

Possession, Ownership, and Freedom

K. Saraswathi Amma's "The Subordinate" and Indira Goswami's "The Offspring" form the second group of stories. Interestingly enough, these stories are written, respectively, by the oldest writer and one of the youngest in *Slate*. Translated into English from Malayalam and Assamese, respectively, these stories are among the most explicitly violent and poignant in the collection. While Binapani Mohanty's Lata experiences the violence of rape and finally challenges the very community that makes her an outcast with the proof of their role in her rape (using her child as a way to rise above the abject conditions of her life), K. Saraswathi Amma's Parukutty kills her daughter as an act of liberation and an escape from the bounds of caste, class, and gendered oppression. In "The Offspring" Damayanti uses abortion as a way of controlling her own sexuality, and in "The Subordinate" Parukutty kills her teenage daughter rather than subject her to sexual and social subordination by her own biological father. Both narratives explore death, murder, and the killing of children as one logical and rational response to the inherited patriarchical and caste-class regulation and oppression of women.

Like "Lata," Indira Goswami's "The Offspring" is also set in rural India; the class and caste structure of an Assamese village forms the social context in which the action occurs. But there is no village community in this story, and even the two women characters—the poor Brahmin widow, Damayanti, and the bedridden wife of the landlord—exist in the margins of the action. The story's primary focus is on the interactions between the landlord, Pitambar Mahajan, and the Brahmin priest, Krishnakanta, and it is through the perspectives of these two male characters that the violent misogyny of their world is conveyed to us. This is a misogyny that conflates sexual desire and procreation with a peculiarly violent form of possession. As they stare at Damayanti's body, her "white flesh . . . look[s] as tempting as the meat dressed and hung up on iron hooks in a butcher's shop" (88). Earlier, the priest had noticed how the childless Pitambar had been "devour[ing a] child with envious eyes" (87). What is possessed in this way can also be discarded with a similar violence and contempt; thus, one of the ways the priest tries to convince Damayanti to marry the landlord and bear his child is by telling her how, as a widow, she is "like a piece of sugarcane, chewed and thrown away" (93). Meanwhile, Pitambar's wife, blamed for not being able to conceive, is seen as "a bundle of bones dumped in a corner of the bed" (89); Krishnakanta even sees her eyes "burning like those of an animal in a dark jungle" (90) and, because they represent a kind of moral judgment, her husband threatens to "scoop [them] out" (94).

Damayanti's choices to control her own sexuality may seem violent to some readers, especially since Goswami is graphic in her accounts of the aborted fetuses. But her choices and decisions are not at the center of the story. The focus is on the layers of violence that surround Damayanti and other women in this social system. The discursive level, the brutal words and the imagery they convey, are inseparable from a way of life in which the danger of physical violence to women is insistently present. The deepest question the story raises concerns the violence that is inherent in an ideology of almost literal possession and consumption of others' bodies, an economy that extends to all relationships. We do not have to strain the imagination much to see the "great pleasure and satisfaction" with which Pitambar Mahajan "would inhale . . . the fresh fragrance of [the] newly harvested paddy" that his tenants bring him every July (92) as essentially continuous with the manic desire that he displays at the end to dig up and retrieve the fetus: "I'll touch that flesh with these hands of mine. He was the scion of my lineage, a part of my flesh and blood! I will touch him!" (99). If Damayanti's resistance to her status as merely a sexual and procreative creature is seen in the light of this more comprehensive image, the political and moral implications of gender resonate outward to include the reified "inner" world of men in this story, where social power and a predatory sexuality inform a perversely masculinist image of selfhood.

K. Saraswathi Amma's "The Subordinate" also points to the densely interwoven meanings of the social and personal worlds, examining the ambiguities of religion and culture.[6] In reenacting the moment of conscious and deliberate rebellion that we saw most starkly in "Lata," K. Saraswathi Amma represents that moment as imbedded in complex images of religious worship, images which are fundamentally gendered. For many Hindu women, Lord Krishna is a very personal, indeed erotic, object of worship. According to legend, he is among other things a sexually playful god, and his sexuality both humanizes him and makes possible a different modality of worship and devotion. The seventeen-year-old Parukutty's fond memory of her first sexual encounter reveals that it happens on Krishnashtami, Lord Krishna's birthday. She has been out gathering flowers for the puja, the worship of Lord Krishna, and the moment of seduction is defined by the multiple meanings of her sexuality. The lawyer, whose name (Gopalan) is another of Lord Krishna's names, plays on the many relationships that a devout but "guileless" young woman might have with the meanings of worship.

> He stood rooted to the spot, attracted by the fragrance of the flowers and the beauty of the girl who held them. "Do you know who you should worship on Ashtami Rohini day?" Parukutty was taken aback by her young master's words and the expression on his face. But she was suffused with a rare kind of inner happiness and said, "I know. Today is Lord Krishna's birthday. I have plucked all these flowers for his worship."
>
> Gopalan Nair moved closer to her. "Then do that. I am also named after Lord Krishna. Worship me. I, too, love flowers." (61)

In Parukutty's mind, there is a not altogether vague connection between the "rare kind of inner happiness" (61) that we have just seen and the "inexplicable joy" that "fill[s] her being" (61) when Gopalan first touches her. She may be anxious, but later, reliving the feeling of "a man's touch for the first time," she "folded her hands . . . and prostrated herself in front of the Lord's idol. Her fervent prayer was, 'Lord, help him grow into a great man. May I be of help to him, not a hindrance'" (61).

Unlike Binapani Mohanty, K. Saraswathi Amma is interested in psychological realism, but readers of "The Subordinate" will miss the meanings of Paru's actions if they are not attentive to the particular cultural (and specifically religious) lenses through which Paru interprets herself and her world. For when the much older Paru Amma decides that she cannot allow her daughter, Lakshmikutty, to be sexually exploited by her father, and thus relegated to a subordinate condition for life, she kills her in front of Lord Krishna, her own "hands joined in prayer" (65). Like the slave mother Sethe in Toni Morrison's *Beloved*,[7] who slits her child's throat to save her from the absolute degradation of slavery, Parukutty's action can be seen as a product of serious moral deliberation. In both cases, the mother relives her own life of subordination and humiliation and decides that, come what may, her daughter shall not endure a similar fate. Toni Morrison's Sethe raises the question of what genuine freedom consists in, of what it means to "claim ownership of [one's] freed self" (95). "Lata" and "The Subordinate" begin to raise the same question and take us beyond purely legal or institutional battles against gender or caste subordination. Simultaneous with this purely political struggle is the struggle to establish the conditions in which choosing and deciding, making and remaking oneself and one's world, are possible not only for a privileged few but for everyone. And a major part of this struggle, these stories suggest, is one of individual and collective imagination, of consciousness, of the shapes and forms that inform and inflect our moral agency. The moment of explicit rebellion, the powerful moment of eruption, is incomplete if it is not seen as leading to this kind of questioning.

Roles, Identities, Visions of Community

The last group of stories, Bani Basu's "Aunty," Meena Alexander's "Grandmother's Letters," Rajee Seth's "Against Myself," and Ajeet Cour's "Dead End," chart the dangers and the possibilities of transforming and going beyond the accepted frameworks of sexual and patriarchal identities. Each story examines the contours of a particular inherited female identity: aunt/widow, grandmother, wife, and sister, and explores the potential for going beyond the formally defined roles by recasting the meanings attached to them. "Aunty" and "Grandmother's Letters" suggest two radically different choices and options for women of a particular generation: total erasure from the landscape of familial ties, or the growth of a politicized gender consciousness through involvement in the nationalist struggle.

Bani Basu's "Aunty" is the only story in this collection that focuses on an elderly (seventy-three-year-old) widow. The author maps the geography and location of widows within the social and familial fabric of small town, middle-class, Indian culture. Gender identity is explored here through a depiction of the relationships that constitute older women as "aunts" and "widows" especially in the context of their being the only survivors of their generation. Unlike most of the other stories, the texture and images of Bani Basu's text are based in the details of conversations, rather than in the natural or physical landscape. By paying close attention to the nuances of the conversations, which provide seemingly irrelevant details about the daily lives of the characters, the reader is able to get a feel for the minute economic and domestic exchanges necessary in maintaining the caste, class, religious, and sexual relations within this intergenerational Bengali household.

The narrative begins with the funeral of the patriarch of the house, Aunty's brother and the father of the five siblings (two sons and three daughters) whose actions toward her constitute the story. The funeral exposes the instability of her position in the household. A child-widow who has mothered her brother's children, she has never legitimately occupied the position of mother. Bani Basu focuses on generational differences in the meanings attached to family, community, and especially home and property. Like Chudamani Raghavan's Brinda and Dhiruben Patel's Kushi, Aunty defines her relation to her family in terms that are outside the economy of material and economic exchange. Her generosity toward her nieces and nephews is revealed in the minute details of the food she cooks for them. She considers all of them "my eyes and my legs." In contrast, Atish, one of the nephews, sees her as "a pod that had outgrown the fruit. With her rheumatic legs, she suddenly looked eighty, now that her brother was dead. Helpless, immobile, like a bundle" (110). Aunty is defined here in relation to her brother—she looks eighty, rather than her actual age of seventy-three because her brother is dead.

The death of the father, Aunty's brother, precipitates discussions of the inheritance of property and its division among the siblings. This is the first moment of her erasure. As each sibling justifies his or her share of the inheritance, the fact that Aunty may inherit as well, or that it might be her home that is being apportioned off, never surfaces. The decision to find a rest home for her is made on the basis of her being "totally alone" (115)—now that her brother has passed away. Thus, the ties of love and affection that actually constitute the day-to-day interactions and relationships between her and the children are forgotten in the process of this decision-making. While the stated reason for this decision is that she is too old to live alone, Bani Basu allows the reader access to the real reasons, which have more to do with the inheritance of the father's property once the old woman is out of the way. Hindu widows have always occupied a liminal space in the context of patriarchal domestic and sexual arrangements.[8] They fall outside the economy of the sexual contract since they are single. "Aunty" is a graphic delineation of the tragic consequences of the social space occupied by widows, those whose gendered identity is constituted outside the parameters of the inherited roles of wife, mother, or daughter.

The story contrasts Aunty's generosity and affection toward her brother's children, whom she considers her own, with their material greed and self-centeredness. Like Dhiruben Patel's Kushi and Chudamani Raghavan's Brinda, Aunty is "sold out" by her family, those nearest and dearest to her. While Kushi and Brinda are daughters responding to the demands of parents, Aunty is betrayed by the very children to whom she has devoted her entire life. When the siblings finally realize the mistake they have made in committing Aunty to a Hindu social service institution and finally acknowledge her as the mother they grew up with, it is too late. Aunty, whose given name, Ruchishila, is mentioned only once in the text, is erased once again along with the particularities of her face, body, gestures, and history, as at the end of the story she actually disappears within a generic group of older, destitute women before our very eyes. The siblings notice that

> Aunty had never been photographed on any occasion. Also, that she was not too thin, nor fat; neither dark, nor fair; her hair was not all gray, nor all black; she hadn't lost all her teeth, nor did she have all of them; she was not too old, but certainly nothing less than old. Actually, she had no identifying mark on her. In fact, she was just an aunt. One of innumerable aunts. Not anyone's mother or father, just an aunt. (124)

It is this erasure, on a number of different levels—psychological, social, familial, and finally physical—that Bani Basu's poignant narrative seeks to trace and outline.

Meena Alexander's "Grandmother's Letters," on the other hand, offers a very different account of the domestic and sexual arrangements and agency of women in the early part of the century in the context of the anticolonial struggle. Along with Rajee Seth's "Against Myself" and Ajeet Cour's "Dead End," this story focuses on the development and exploration of the meanings attached to the growing consciousness and experience of womanhood in historical and social circumstances that limit and regulate such consciousness. Both the grandmother in Meena Alexander's story and the sister in Ajeet Cour's narrative are caught in the midst of larger political upheavals. The wife in Rajee Seth's story is perhaps the most familiar to Western readers—she is a "modern," urban, middle-class protagonist, and her trajectory raises questions about the hypocrisy underlying the everyday, well-intentioned behavior of progressive men, leading us to ask how masculinity must be transformed in a world which seeks to eradicate the injustices of the patriarchal subjugation of women.

In "Grandmother's Letters," the only story written originally in English, Meena Alexander provides an archaeology of the subjective states of the narrator's grandmother, Kanda, during her involvement in the independence movement in India of the 1920s and 1930s.

> My grandmother was imprisoned in the mountains. I think she understood the loneliness of a woman's body as she sat there, looking out at the elaichi tree, brown now in the bitter season. She was just twenty-seven when the British imprisoned her. (26)

This beginning identifies the threads interwoven in the narrative: the articulation of specifically gendered emotions and desires, the loneliness of certain political choices, as well as of physical imprisonment; and the identification and location of the narrator, who we are told was born fourteen years after the death of her grandmother. The story centers on the narrator's discovery of her grandmother's letters and the gradual unraveling of the emotional contradictions, costs, and expectations of women who were freedom fighters in the early days of the anticolonial struggle. The letters themselves are written over the space of three years (1929–1931) and document Kanda's imprisonment, her husband's subsequent imprisonment, their separation as one of the costs of involvement in the struggle, and finally the death of Kanda's father, the narrator's great-grandfather.

The narrative weaves back and forth between images of looking out at the world through barred windows and the promise of freedom, liberation, and the "paradise" beyond it. As in so many of the stories in this collection, the regenerative qualities of nature—flowers in bloom, the landscape, and water—suggest the expansiveness and strength of convictions (in this case fighting for liberation from British colonialism) even under the most abject circumstances of imprisonment. Kanda writes her husband:

> You have a small window that looks out on the hills. Unlock the bars with your gaze, deceive the distances till they come swarming off the purple hills hung with jacaranda bloom. Let the distances uphold you. A stream, a bright blade of grass. . . . (28)

Meena Alexander's text is filled with images of blood, birds in flight, the danger of snakes, and the stability and invincibility of the mountains and hills; together they attempt an emotional cartography of Kanda's beliefs and convictions. Four generations of women form the backbone of this narrative, though the primary relationship is that of the narrator's grandparents, especially as imagined ("is she like myself inventing a great deal?" [27]) and interpreted by the narrator through Kanda's letters. Loneliness and a certain stark sorrow seem to tie the generations of women together. Through Kanda's political activism and commitment to the struggle, Meena Alexander manages to create a vivid portrait of nationalist women in the Gandhian movement—women who felt acutely the sexual and domestic costs and contradictions of being women fighting for the nation. Such choices were both joyous and costly.

Like Bani Basu's narrative, which marks the passing of the patriarch as an important moment for access to genuine knowledge, Meena Alexander's story ends with the funeral of Kanda's father (the patriarch), and a careful, detailed exploration of the emotions attached to his passing away—the ways in which he is mourned by his wife, daughter, and granddaughter (the narrator's mother). Inflections of caste and class complicate Kanda's political choices, and ideologies of equality and self-sufficiency motivate her involvement in the struggle. Thus, loneliness is explored on another level—that of distance from the members of her caste and community, who throw away money on rituals to maintain and consolidate their status in society. In some ways this is a very "modern" story, depicting the psychological development of a gendered political consciousness and of the process of becoming a woman in the midst of public engagement in the nationalist struggle.

Psychic awareness of the slow death of creativity amid the contradictions and loneliness of middle-class, urban marital and domestic life shapes Rajee Seth's character Ruchi in "Against Myself." This is the story which may seem most familiar to North American readers. It is built around the development of a writer's consciousness of the gendered exchanges involved in integrating and nourishing the parts of her self that seem to matter the most: her writing, and her relation to her husband, Shyam. Interestingly enough, this is the one story in *Slate* that revolves around a male-female relationship almost to the exclusion of any sense of community, or even any marker of place, region, or extended family. Shyam and Ruchi spend their honeymoon in Simla—the sole geographical marker in this story. While this is a story about a particular woman's psychic development, it also works on a more general level, identifying the costs for women of male-female relationships built on sexual, affectional, and domestic exchanges within the patriarchal frames of male possessiveness and ownership.

Rajee Seth begins by drawing attention to the bond between men, which often colonizes and erases the responsibilities of men to women. Shyam nurtures his older colleague Devji because his creativity cannot be allowed to die and yet, Ruchi realizes, he has watched her "waste away" (50) as a writer without so much as an acknowledgment. Ruchi's sensibility and her awareness of the compromises she has made are encapsulated in her characterization of her wifely relationship as the maintenance of "Calm, but at a cost!" (51).

Through a series of interchanges between the couple, the story moves slowly but surely to Ruchi's final recognition that forcing Shyam to acknowledge and support her creativity as a writer would be like being "at war with myself. Against myself!" (56). After all, every time she brings up her writing, Shyam responds by making love to her: "exchanging one kind of bliss for another!" (51–2). Ruchi thinks to herself,

> Only women, perhaps, can be so stupid as to start toasting their literary dreams on the warmth of a love that is just kindling. But when some lines of poesy strumming up in my mind made it to my lips, Shyam

> promptly sealed them there. Instead he let loose a trail of fire on my body. (51)

Thus, even within the context of a liberal marriage seemingly built on personal choice rather than exchanges between families, even in the context of both partners aspiring to be writers (Shyam is a well-known journalist), Rajee Seth's narrative raises pertinent questions about the gendered ideology even of "progressive" men and about the use of sexual interchange and the trappings of middle-class domesticity to possess and control women.

Finally, Ruchi burns her notebooks of poems to punish Shyam—to communicate with a gesture something she had never been able to say with words, because he never took her words seriously. She recognizes immediately, however, that she has in fact punished herself. Shyam says that he cannot bear to see her torn between her work and her love for him. But Ruchi is now clear about his motives.

> Something hardened inside me. He did not like my being split into pieces, but he was the one who had divided me thus. He had cut me into two by not accepting one part of me. One, secure for himself, and the other, left to rot within me! What he really wanted was to possess me. Totally! But for that he would have to accept me as a whole first. Did he even know that? (55)

Like a number of the women in *Slate*, Ruchi recognizes the costs of transforming and recasting inherited gender roles and identities. Ruchi is not a "traditional" wife; she is not subjected to physical or overt psychological abuse, and she seems to be outside the expectations of familial and communal networks. In fact, she is cherished sexually. She is not, however, taken seriously as a writer, as someone who labors for reasons other than to serve her partner. The only form of labor Shyam recognizes is the kind that is directed toward him. This too is a form of violence, Ruchi comes to realize. Thus, one of the most significant questions Rajee Seth raises in "Against Myself" is about the necessary transformations of masculinity that must take place for women to be able to write themselves into existence—to make choices as individuals, and to live by those choices.

Finally, Ajeet Cour's young, nameless heroine in "Dead End" suggests the practicality and even the possibility of overcoming familial, caste, and political divisions. The story sketches a utopian relationship between a young woman and a young man defined as her enemy and accused of murdering her brother. The creation of a "new" family through caring and nurturing practices between adversaries offers a vision of the social that goes beyond the artificial social and ideological divisions of contemporary Indian society.

Ajeet Cour's young protagonist has an innocence and an active, emotionally rich psychic life that are often at odds with the overt gendered messages of society. Like Wajida Tabassum's Chamki, Ajeet Cour's heroine questions the received hierarchies of caste and class:

> I could never understand how Kambohs were low caste, because their traditional occupation used to be dyeing clothes. How can people who make ordinary, drab-looking clothes come alive with rainbow colors, be low caste? For that matter, how can people who create beauty by weaving cloth, by dyeing it, by stitching it; by transforming hard, foul-smelling dead hides into beautiful footwear and bags; by molding ordinary clay into beautiful pots and pans, be low caste? (68)

This helps us see her imagination as truly unusual, especially given the material conditions of her life. Ajeet Cour weaves a lyrical, almost magical, tale of death, mourning, hope, and possibility amid the most violent and abject of circumstances: an ethnic and religious war that has led to the deaths of hundreds of people. Instead of the most overt self-definitions based on social caste and gender, this young woman, who is in the process of coming to terms with the murder of her brother, chooses to judge herself and others on the basis of their "deeds and achievements and human values" (68).

A story set in a poor village in rural Punjab, "Dead End" creates a sense of the village community as an extended family in which members of the community, including the police and shopkeepers, look after and protect the mother and daughter who have been hurled into a "yawning abyss" (69) with the death of Kewal, the son and brother. However, this is also the very same community that hunts for and defines as enemy the young man who becomes the protagonist's brother.

> After the first rude shock, I realized that his eyes were very innocent.
>
> I tried to relate those eyes to his face. Every muscle in it was tense with terror. Even his short, curly beard was trembling with fear. (70)

This recognition of innocence and fear leads Ajeet Cour's protagonist to decisions that would make no sense in the prevailing moral economy, one of war, division, and religious hatred. Instead, she sees herself "like a hen, protecting her helpless, wingless chick . . . like a mother protecting her wounded son" (72). The young man refers to her as his sister, while she takes care of him and shields him to the end. It is his suffering that allows her to see him as her brother, Kewal, who was also shot in the same way. Thus, Ajeet Cour sets up an economy of human interactions in which exchange no longer indicates an inevitable hierarchy. This is a domestic economy in which inherited caste-specific roles of mother, sister, and brother are remade through the everyday, ordinary gestures of kindness and nurturance. Of all the stories in *Slate*, this is the one that fundamentally transforms the intimate relations of domestic and sexual exchange, suggesting that the *practices* of mothering and the *labor* of caretaking are what make one a mother or a sister—not some inherited, abstract, codified notion of the role of a mother or sister. The final moment in the story underlines this, when the mother hearing gunfire, rushes out and pleads with the world to not kill her son—the young man, the so-called enemy, that her daughter has protected and nurtured.

Ajeet Cour suggests new possibilities for cross-gender interaction and relationships; she also ends by suggesting a community of women drawn together by their common perception of an emotional and affective economy that transcends imposed social divisions and barriers. In the context of contemporary India, where the experience of everyday social life is threatened by communal, ethnic, and religious tensions, Ajeet Cour's vision is a healing one.

Autonomy, Collectivity, and the Labor of the Imagination

While the authors of these stories describe various kinds of violence and dispossession that define women's lives, we have argued that a feminist reading of these stories would be partial and inaccurate without an appreciation of the extent to which these women are moral and indeed historical agents, the subjects of their own lives. It is through their personal and collective agency that the political reality of gender becomes most forcefully articulated. These stories are not about inarticulate cries in the dark. They mark complexly determined spaces in which a critical awareness is developed, choices are made, meanings are analyzed and reformulated—in short, where lives are lived. And in these subjective choices are outlined new positive values that help the reader see—through the implied contrast—the stark reality of gender relations, and the dispossession, powerlessness, and violence of everyday indignities.

At the end of "The Subordinate" Parukutty, having taken her daughter's life with Lord Krishna as her witness, speaks with a new sense of her dignity and personal worth. She announces her name calmly, claiming a new stance, a different relationship to her actions and her life: "My name is Paru Amma," she says to the Commissioner. "Earlier, everyone used to call me Parukutty. Now people will recognize me only if you refer to me as Paru Amma, the sweeper of the temple" (66). Her identity as "sweeper of the temple" aligns her with the Lord who was "born to protect the helpless and reestablish dharma" (65). *Dharma* is the just moral order; and it is with this vision both of herself and the world she is working to create that Paru Amma helps us see retrospectively the precise moral dimensions of her history. The new value—the assertion of herself as the author of her actions, responsible for her self—derives from a new definition of her personhood, a definition that gestures beyond the patriarchal and caste-ridden society in which she lives.

Even in the most abject of social conditions, what Paru Amma claims for herself at the end of the story is autonomy, the freedom to choose what she can and will value. This is what Wajida Tabassum's Chamki suggests when she tells her mother that she must accept the gifts from the rich mistress because "we have little choice," but that that does not constrain her to feel grateful: "please don't feel so happy when you take them" (39). One's worth as a person is not exhausted by one's social conditions and one's material deprivation, characters like Chamki insist. This is the vision developed as well in the bold outlines of Lata's image at the end of the story as she stands with her bastard son, claiming him as not only her own but also as the source of a new dimension of social meaning. Lata's assertion of her choice is directed against the values her community espouses toward a radically new future: the child "fl[ies] up into the clouds" (49) to suggest that he understands and knows what his mother's vision implies. Autonomy involves reasoning and moral deliberation, the claiming of ownership of one's actions and choices. Lata and her son together provide a social and political vision as well, of a new kind of ownership in which the outcast reclaims her right to belong by claiming to remake her community and its values.

It would be reductive to see in this vision an unresolvable opposition between the needs of the individual and those of her community or society. The society Lata and her son seek is the one that Damayanti might yearn for as well. It is certainly the one that Brinda's and Kushi's utopian images of free, unfettered creativity suggest when they are developed as ideals of equal, nonexploitative interpersonal relationships. A just society is one that not only protects the moral autonomy of the individual, but in fact enables and nurtures it. Justice cannot be reduced to an abstract formula, since it is inevitably composed of values and of human relationships that embody and deepen these values.

As the new figuration of the hitherto impossible community in Ajeet Cour's story suggests, beyond the distortions and disfigurations of gender, caste, and ethnic violence lies the possibility of a renewed feminist imagination. In "Dead End" it is through attentiveness to emotions and feelings of loss, sorrow, and suffering that the young woman is able to imagine and practice familial and communal relations based on dignity, kindness, and reciprocity. Ajeet Cour introduces a different cognitive register for the definition and redefinition of the collective. In the same breath, she foregrounds the agency of poor, low-caste, rural women in defining this new nonhierarchical collective. This suggests how the stories in *Slate* might be read as continuous with third-world feminist political projects.

One of the major contributions of third-world feminist projects has been their insistence on placing poor and dispossessed women at the center of analysis and organizing. While political and legal equality has always been a significant aspect of third-world feminist demands, questions of the effects of poverty and dispossession; lack of adequate food, shelter, and health and educational resources; and the violence that these material conditions engender, have been at the center of women's movements in countries like India. One of the challenges third-world feminists face, not unlike those faced by feminists in the first world, is to elaborate a vision of community that takes into account both the reality of deprivation and violence and the possibility of reciprocity, cooperation, and nonexploitative social exchange. *The Slate of Life* invites and encourages its readers to take part in the collective labor demanded by this radical vision. It is a labor—fundamentally of the imagination—whose possibility poses the most difficult of cross-cultural challenges. It forces readers to trade empty and fashionable slogans of cultural otherness for a genuinely reciprocal and honest exchange with the text, and potentially with lives, experiences, and values that are radically different from their own.

Notes

We would like to thank Neeti Madan, Deba P. Patnaik, and Paul St. Pierre for their comments and suggestions.

1. It is important to acknowledge the work of Kali for Women, India's first women's publishing house, founded in 1984. The stories in *Slate* were chosen by Kali for Women and represent an ongoing effort to translate women's writings from different Indian languages. Other Kali collections include *Truth Tales: Contemporary Stories by Women Writers of India*, also republished by The Feminist Press; *In Other Words:*

New Writing by Indian Women, selected by Urvashi Butalia and Ritu Menon; *Inner Spaces, New Writing by Women from Kerala*, ed. K. M. George et al. (forthcoming); and *Eclipsed Worlds, A Collection of Hindi Short Stories by Women*, trans. Jasjit Purewal (forthcoming). See also *The Inner Courtyard: Stories by Indian Women*, ed. Lakshmi Holmstrom (London, Virago Press, 1990).

2. The most complete literary history of Indian women writers, written by Susie Tharu and K. Lalita in *Women Writing in India: 600 B.C. to the Present, Vol. 2* (New York: The Feminist Press, 1993), frames contemporary women's literature in terms of women writing the nation. Briefly, Tharu and Lalita trace the genealogy of the 1970s women's movement in India and the corresponding emergence of feminist creativity and criticism, to (1) the issues of caste and communalism that emerge from the Gandhian Swadeshi (literally "of-one's-own-country") movement (1905–1908), which was a central part of the anti-colonial struggle, (2) issues of gender and class raised within the context of the socialist Progressive Writers' Associations in the mid-1930s, and (3) the liberal women's movement in the 1920s and 1930s, with its focus on electoral reforms.

3. *The Slate of Life* raises some fundamental questions relating to the translation of regional literature into and within the national space of "Indian literature." For a discussion of the difficulties and complexities involved in defining the entity "Indian literature" as not just the mere sum of its regional parts, see Aijaz Ahmad, "'Indian Literature': Notes towards the Definition of a Category," in his *In Theory: Classes, Nations, Literatures* (London: Verso, 1992), 243–285.

4. In writing this introduction, one of our major concerns is that the women in the stories in *Slate* not be read either as exotic natives or as mere victims of patriarchal, class, and caste violence. While the women in *Slate* cannot be assimilated into some abstract feminist narrative of liberation, we have tried to draw attention to the ways in which they make and remake their own worlds, surviving and indeed fighting practices of objectification and victimization. In fact, the more immediate context of the marketing and consumption of literary, commercial, and popular-artistic images of India in the West, as well as the real gaps in public knowledge about the relationship between Indian regional and national audiences and readerships need to be taken into account in reading the stories in *Slate*.

5. For a more developed discussion of the links between experience and identity see Satya P. Mohanty, "The Epistemic Status of Cultural Identity: On *Beloved* and the Postcolonial Condition," *Cultural Critique* 24 (Spring 1993), 41–80, and Chandra Talpade Mohanty, "Feminist Encounters, Locating the Politics of Experience," in *Destabilizing Theory, Contemporary Feminist Debates*, ed. M. Barrett and A. Phillips (Cambridge and Oxford: Polity Press, 1992) 74–92.

6. A selection of K. Saraswathi Amma's fiction, *Stories from a Forgotten Feminist*, translated and with an introduction by Jancy James is forthcoming from Kali for Women.

7. Toni Morrison, *Beloved* (New York: Knopf, 1987).

8. "The Widow: A New Incarnation" in Tharu and Lalita's introduction, "The Twentieth Century: Women Writing the Nation," in *Women Writing in India*, Vol. 2, 106–109.

Meena Alexander

Grandmother's Letters

1

My grandmother was imprisoned in the mountains. I think she understood the loneliness of a woman's body as she sat there, looking out at the elaichi tree, brown now in the bitter season. She was just twenty-seven when the British imprisoned her. She sat on the floor by the window and a wild light fell upon her.

She touched her thin belly, dark, utterly unscarred. She wondered if she would ever be let out of prison. If she would ever bear children. She saw the gray rocks of the Deccani mountains. She smelled the bitter grasses burned by the goatherds on the slopes outside her barred window.

She stoops in the light. She picks up her pen and her paper. Her hair is tied back with a red ribbon. It is the very same ribbon that grandfather used to tie up the letters she wrote him when he was imprisoned. Many years after his death I discovered the letters in an old biscuit box, in the attic of the Tiruvana house.

The black syllables flash in my mind's eye. I hold them for an instant. Her pen is dry. She shakes it. The ink spurts. I repeat her letters as I write. I sound them out. I will not slip into the black flood of time. I will save myself.

How carefully grandmother uses her pen. And paper is scarce. She writes:

"Let the rice grow."

"Let the children play in the sunlight."

"There is mud on your cheek, beloved."

The last is addressed to grandfather, who is underground. She does not know if he will ever receive her letters. Barely knowing what she writes, she adds:

"The koel sings in its own light. Those who listen will never forget."

Did she really hear the dun colored bird cry? Or is she like myself, inventing a great deal? How I wish I had known grandmother. She was dead fourteen years by the time I was born. By the time I was born in 1951, India was independent, a republic already for three and a half years.

I see grandmother stand on a small wooden crate at the Pakeezah steps. It is early in the morning, the day before Gandhi's Salt March. Her sari tucked into her waist, she addresses the fisherfolk. The crate wobbles a little as she speaks but she does not falter.

"Collect salt water in your palms!"

I hear her say.

"Let the great heat of the sun make salt for you."

"Let the Britishers see how against nature it is to prevent us."

The crowd claps. She steps off the crate holding her pallu in her hand. She is nervous. She tugs at the red and white threads with her thumb and forefinger. Her hair blows in the sunlight.

A tall, thin figure in white rushes out of the crowd. He embraces her, then overcome by shyness stands utterly still at her side, head bent. I cannot see his face.

It's grandfather! What is she saying to him? I wish I could hear. A child runs up with a garland. Grandmother stoops and the golden ring falls over her neck. Her mouth is in the shadow. Grandfather still stands there. Behind them, in the distance, I can see the dark waters of the Arabian Sea.

Grandfather stands there and stares at her. It's the very first time he has set eyes on her. For years he had heard of her, her marches, her speeches, her nonviolent demonstrations. He has even published some of her little texts in the journal he runs. Now he stands by her side, in the blazing light, drinking in her presence. Side by side they stand, each looking forward, too nervous, too shy to look into the other's eyes.

Someone tugs at grandfather's arm. He has a meeting to attend in the next town. Grandmother stands there, for an instant, in utter solitude, bereft of this stranger she already loves. A pigeon casts its shadow on her head. She touches her own cheek, her eyes shut, as if feeling her flesh for the first time. Then the crowd engulfs her.

Three months after this first meeting with grandfather, grandmother was in prison, charged by the British with disturbing the peace. When they let her out after two and a half years in the mountain cell, she was twenty-nine years old, thinner than ever, thankful at last for the ordinary light.

There were blue rings under her eyes, dark smudges under her pupils. Though no one knew it, it was the start of her blindness.

The day of her release, she returned to the Pakeezah steps. Overcome by emotion, she wept a little as she stood there. Her hands trembled in the air. Her crimson pallu flashed in the slight wind. There was salt in her eyes. Grandfather stood right in front of her, next to the leaders of the movement, listening intently. A few weeks later they were married. It took him three years to nurse her back to health. In prison she had refused most of the food set before her and had lived off wild rice and water.

2

Seven years ago I discovered some of grandmother's letters crammed into a biscuit tin in my mother's house. My mother was her only child. This grandmother, Kanda, unlike my other grandmother, Mariamma, had died long before my birth. I put the letters together dreaming a little. Most of the letters were written after her release from prison.

I remember the first letter I read. It was addressed directly to grandfather. She was at home now and it was he who was imprisoned.

Kuruchiethu
Tiruvana
January 16, 1929

. . . You have a small window, Kuruvilla, that looks out on the hills. Unlock the bars with your gaze, deceive the distances till they come swarming off the purple hills hung now with jacaranda bloom. Let the distances uphold you. A stream, a bright blade of grass. Even if the stream is dried and puffs dust rather than water, even if the blade is rusty with death. I am sure from your descriptions that the room they keep you in is close, very close to where I was. Perhaps the bars are identical. Perhaps we look out and see the very same bird, dust colored, a speckle of blood on its beak, turning in the sunlight at the rim of the hill.

As time passed things became harder for her. She kept going to political meetings. Her friend, Balamaniamma the writer, was her mainstay in those years.

Kuruchiethu
Tiruvana
April 21, 1930

K.

I am not even sure anymore what I say. There is some desolation in me I cannot touch with my own fingers. I need you.

At the meeting Dinesh said, "Gandhi wants him to come to Wardah, as soon as he's out."

Your press is running. Each night the pamphlets, still wet with ink, pass from hand to hand. A long line of text, piercing the alien world. The police haven't found out the source, though they've been nosing around.

Balamani and I worked on the last one together: "Liberated India and Free Women," we called it. She had a dream: as day breaks, all the women in the new world clasp hands, rise from sullen earth like sunbirds. "Our flesh is light," she told me that night as she worked, inky, covered in sweat. "You are the morning star," she wrote. "All stars since the birth of this universe! Your chains lie useless. They drop through the waters."

There is something more to the dream: in the distance, through the waters, speed English ships, mere tin vessels, their flags limp, speeding to the damp cold little island.

I teased Balamani later: "So many stars! You'll empty out the night sky!" But she takes her dreams quite seriously and sat gazing out of the window, at the stubble, barbed wire Bhaskar had strung to keep the milk cows away from the strawberry patch. I could not tell what she was looking at. You know that faraway gaze of hers . . . one barely knows if she's listening.

I do love her very much, but she has been a little strange of late. She seems obsessed by the Qutubshahi emperor, the last one. "I'm convinced," she says to me the other night, "that his madness (crawling up the stairs and all that) was a response to British invasion. Remember his quest took a form. A vanished bird. A dot of blood on its beak."

I left it at that. In any case she did not really want a reply. It was dark and the mango trees made huge black umbrellas that kept the moon out. I thought the foundations of our house shook a little. The water rats were playing in the strawberry patch. I could tell by the silver glint in their tails. So we just sat there, in silence.

3

Grandmother kept going by herself, though, to all the family gatherings. One of her letters tells of an elaborate christening her cousin had arranged for her three-month-old daughter. It is hardly surprising that grandmother found the displays of wealth unsuitable. She wrote grandfather about it, in some detail.

Kuruchiethu
Tiruvana
September 29, 1930

Accamma's daughter's naming ceremony was done with such splendor, you might have thought us in Babylon or some such pagan city. Silver, a huge city, mound on mound, from candlesticks to pepper pots. Porcelain, glittering in the sunlight. Lace tablecloths! And on the floor, for guests to eat off, piles of banana leaves. A whole forest wasted, to name a child!

They are terribly rich and hold onto their estates with an iron hand. I hear the father of the child wields a gun. They carry out floggings on the land. Five elephants in the procession from the church, all from the personal herd, the grandmother took great care to point out to me.

The father's brother was in Western dress. Can you imagine, the ignominy of wearing that dress in times like ours! I couldn't bear to look at his polished shoes. He came straight to me.

"There you are, Kanda!" I've no idea how he found me out. "So you don't believe in British rule, hah?" I should have slapped him then and there in front of all the guests. But he moved away smartly, to the other side of the great copper urn they were serving tea from. I think it's all imported from Belgium or some such place. Then, as I was helping myself to some papaya, he leaned over the sugar bowl, grinning from ear to ear. "Your husband's in jail, isn't he?!"

I almost dropped my plate. I sat myself in a corner after that and did not move. It was a kind of rage that would not let me breathe. Through the window, I could see the servants' children, mouths covered with flies, shoving and pushing to get at the heap of banana leaves that were tossed out. Kuru, I felt sick at heart. Thank god Mara didn't come with me.

When I got home, the house was all peaceful, the curtains drawn. Mara was asleep under her little white sheet. I sat down at your desk and signed over the rice fields we had decided on. The Bhoodan movement will make good use of them. There's such a terrible hunger for land now. Sometimes, I feel that this house we live in, and all the ancestral property, are like a great millstone, a granite ring about my neck. I know one day I shall perish because of it: the rooms I inhabit will be mist. My womb full of blackberries, fit for the birds of paradise.

"You and I will live in a field," I was going to say, then realized that in that world, we will not need our bodies either. Our flesh and blood is a mere contingency, bound to this earth.

I hear Mara cry. Where will she be, I wonder, in that world? And suddenly I am full of fear. Is the sheet over her mouth? Is she on a cliff, hanging by her nails, in a nightmare? A puff of black wind?

I found her wandering through the fig patch one morning drawn by the wet sticky smell of the frangipani. She was there, almost before I could get to her, poking her fist into a snake hole. I slapped her hard, I was so scared. She burst into tears. "The big rats make the hole, then the cobra goes in. It'll bite Mara!" I picked her up and ran away with her, feeling the wind on my heels. Then slowed down, out of breath, by the jacaranda tree. I set her in the swing and pushed her high in the air. Through her eyes I saw the great blue sky. There were bees in the honeysuckle that twines around the tree trunks and golden dragonflies in the lilies. Even the dry brown leaves were buzzing with life. "More, more," she cried out and I pushed her higher and higher, till I too seemed to be flying through the brilliant blue air, into paradise.

It's all there, Kuru, I want to say to you. It's all already there. Paradise, I mean. And this terrible oppression of mind and body that we struggle against is a passage, a birth. I must stop now, my love. I shall write again, very soon. Much much love.

Kanda

P.S. Yacub says that Gandhi is planning a visit to Tiruthankur. I must make sure he has somewhere to stay. Perhaps even here? He asked about you, Yacub says. They are busy now with the work in Gujarat.

K

4

Six months later, the day before her birthday, she felt herself slip into her own eyes, fall through her face in loneliness. Or so I thought, reading her lines. But her humor held her up and that fat Chinamma who haunted her, dropping in and out of grandmother's days. I could hear grandmother's voice so clearly, perhaps with the slight distortion my own voice has as I listen to it.

Kuruchiethu
Tiruvana
February 17, 1931

Yesterday I stood in front of the oval mirror and looked at my eyes. They were so huge, so formless. So black. I picked up the stick of kajal Chinna had given me. Frivolity in hard times, my love! Rimming around the sad flesh. Making boundaries. But I stood there and did nothing but bite my lips. "No, I won't do up my eyes," I said. "Let them be. When I'm dead, let the photographers do it!" What a stupid thing to say, my darling.

But I'm funny these days. I wash my face only in well water. And hardly use soap. And wear white, for days on end till Chinamma says I look like a widow! Tomorrow, I turn thirty.

Kuruchiethu
Tiruvana
March 19, 1931

Chinamma was wearing those wooden clogs she always wears and made a terrible clatter on the marble floor. I embraced her. She smelled of fresh soap. She is like an older sister to me, Kuru. She scolded me, for my hair hung in shreds and had not been oiled, because my lips were bitten. She insisted I come with her the next evening to address the college women in Kozhencheri. She forced me to accept. Even mother was glad I was getting out of the house. Chinamma stayed, ate some fried bitter gourd. She is curing her blood, she says, though only the lord knows what might be up with her blood and what the bitter gourd will do for it. But she has a vaidyan she sees in Kottayam. She follows all his instructions most faithfully.

The college is up on a hill. You've been there, a small whitewashed building overhung with jasmine. I was very eager to meet the women again. Many of them were satyagrahis. I still remember fifty of us, lying on that very road, in the dust, our red-and-white saris tied end to end, the knots bursting through the dust. Our bodies warm and alive, laid in the dust. "The British truck will not pass! Oppression will not last!" we chanted. It seems funny now, in a strange way. Not the passion, but the utter dispossession of self needed to lie on the road. Our passive resistance. I remember how hot my mouth felt. And how pale the white butterfly above me seemed to be, melting into the sunlight. The British were shouting something in the distance. The road trembled with their boots.

After a while Chinamma said she had to get herself a drink of toddy before the meeting and that I should walk up alone. They would be waiting for me. It was a long stretch of road. Soon the houses were all left behind. Even the small, red brick schools. There was just the dusty field, purple now, in the darkness. I could hear my own footsteps. It was unnerving. Like hearing one's own heartbeat. On and on I walked. My tongue felt so dry. Then I started to run. I saw thornbushes that I did not remember seeing before. They had tiny red berries, like drops of blood. I felt like plucking one, to cool my tongue as I ran, but it was dark, and I could not tell if there was poison in that fruit or not. When I finally got to the college, I felt as if I had run an eternity. My ankles were scratched and swollen. I could not stop panting.

5

There was nothing exaggerated about the next letter. Nothing dreamlike. It was as precise as grandmother could make it. It was hardly her fault that she was struggling to spell out feelings that lay outside the ordinary territory of her days. A nothingness within . . . perhaps it had something to do with her father's imminent death.

Tiruvana
May 7, 1931

I watch the grass turn yellow in the rock crevices. People move about me, Kuruvilla, but I have no body of my own. Nothing to grasp. A hollowness at the heart of me. Like the passion fruit we saw together in the hills the year before we married. The vine clawing the air, perfectly tooled; the skin golden, the freckles so smooth on its green globe one wanted to lick it. But through a hole near the stalk all the stuff had dribbled out: seeds, flesh, juice. And it hung on the vine, by the blue mountains, a bell, utterly hollow, not fruit, just skin of fruit, deceiving all the world.

It's weariness, my darling. But where does it come from? I can hardly tell anymore. I am ashamed of speaking like this of myself, and you in your straitened condition, bound in a small dusty room. But you have asked me to speak, and so I do.

Tiruvana
No date

Yacub must have told you. Father is growing steadily worse. He breathes with great difficulty. His lips turn dry and he chokes; cries out as if iron were crushing his ribs. Mara doesn't go near him anymore. She's afraid. Or perhaps even wants him to die. Last night, I could tell he was listening to the bats in the jamun tree. But when mother came with her Bible, he refused to hear. I think he needs to see you. I tell him, as he lies there, his eyes clamped tight, all about your doings. How you are eating a little now, what you read and write, who else is in prison with you, how Gandhi speaks of you.

Sometimes, when the black seeds drop in the air or the jamun splatters its fruit, father seems to breathe more easily. His nails are growing dry and yellow. Mother, with her nose in the Bible, like a huge warthog, hardly moving yet shouting constantly to one servant or another, bring the fried cucumbers, hot compress, prayer book, bell, bowl. And poor father, laid out rigid in that bed, groaning. There's very little the doctors can do for him. It's as if mother must constantly shout out these petty commands to stop her soul up. She cannot conceive of life without father. I fear for her.

It would be like lacking a foot or an arm. Or losing her silken garb and suddenly finding her body in rags. She cannot face herself, nor herself in the world without his presence. So she shouts and fills up the time, or oils poor Mara's hair without stopping. "It'll all fall off, mother. For pity. For Christ's sake!" I cried at her the other day.

The lamps are lit in the dining room. The curtains have blown open. Mother has roused herself and is setting out the silver dishes. I can smell the starched white cloth from where I sit. I think it's because the bishop has promised to come. He wants to see father. I can see mother open her mouth. She is wiping her mouth with her handkerchief. I am so scared she will call out for me. Mara's asleep, my darling. Sometimes at night she cries out. Then I put my cheek by hers and she tucks her arm around my neck. It hardly goes all the way around so she squeezes herself against me. She smells of straw and honey as she sleeps, her mouth wet with milk.

I didn't tell you that as I ran, panting, up that dusty road to the college, a song came into my mind. Nothing whatsoever to do with my talk, as far as I can tell. I think mother used to sing it, ages ago. Or it might have been aunt Sara, poor mad Sara found drowned in a well.

Glistening silk
the color of milk
decking the bride!
Who'll bind up the shroud?
Mama, mama, I'll
come for a ride!

The song has a lovely lilt to it. But it's terrifying. You know that mother keeps her wedding sari in the teak chest. That she will be wrapped in it, when she's borne out of the house? "There are many rooms in my father's house." Kuru, forgive me. Forgive me, darling. She's calling out for me. And I hear the bishop's walking stick on the granite steps.

September 2, 1931

Already, his death is here, living with us. It knows us. And because it's father's death, we welcome it, a kinsman, a twin, known only at the rare moment of passage. I realize now, Kuruvilla, that I have absolutely no religious faith, but I acknowledge my father's death. It troubles the air. It teases the light. The leaves blacken around it. Last night father sipped a little wine and seemed almost happy . . .

Father is more peaceful now and sleeps at night.

His death has settled into the house. The huge iron pots of boiling water we keep at his bedside to help him breathe seem immovable yet part of the ordinary world. Kutan stands by him all afternoon, fanning him.

Now and then, father opens his eyes. In some strange way, he seems to be filled with love. As if his dark blood had fled the wound and light from another shore were pouring in. Bathed in that light, everything is unfamiliar. His bed, the books, spitting bowl, even mother's hand.

Yesterday he raised his fingers and touched her wedding ring. That tiny gold millstone at her knuckle. Tried to say something. But mother fled. I heard her weep from afar. Now she has taken to walking through the pepper vines, ivory cane in hand. Mara follows her, tugging at her hem. It's as if mother does not want to reenter the house. Yesterday she pointed out a swallow to me. It clung to a pepper vine. "It's come from the other side of death, Kanda," she said to me, pointing with the stick. I barely know what she thinks. Yet she's more lucid than before, and all my anger has vanished.

His death leaps with him. They swing from bough to bough. Little boys who would steal gooseberries. Crying out as the air rushes to their skins.

My father dancing with death, Kuru.

Now, nothing but the stench of the old body.

I hid in the bathroom. I heard the hearse clatter down the gravel path. I walked, gravely, as befitting a fatherless child. I buried my head in a hole the gardener had dug. I bit the dust, beneath the gooseberry roots.

Tonight, I enter another hole. No sounds come out of my mouth. It's all a great wind, whirling, unfixing the elements. Father's clothes, juba, dhoti, even his skin, unwrapped and whirling as if all the air in the hole were sucked out with a giant breath. His skin rolls off. It stops at his toe bones: five delicate flowers, blue-petaled, perfect, out of which a great scent rises.

Leaves fall on my head. In that darkness, his flesh vanishes wholly. I bend, to protect my mouth from the wind. I touch a blue flower and find a tiny foot. I tug and tug, feeling my own skin soldered there, breathing so hard I think I will die. My mouth is horribly open, yet I hear nothing but the gasping wind.

Suddenly, the whirlwind ceases. I find I can pull my flesh away. It does not burn as if cut by a red-hot iron. I lie on my back, breathing ever so gently. In my arms, a little child, Mara. Holding her by the waist, I clamber out of the silent hole, lie down on the damp grass, utterly spent.

There are wild bees about us, in her wet tangled hair, in my armpits. Red ants crawl over us. Grasshoppers, their wings drenched with light, all over our eyelids.

She sucks and sucks at my breast. Milk flows out, over the tiny grass blades, the pebbles, and will not stop. Enough for the whole world. Her tiny heart beats hard.

The British are planning large scale repressions, flogging, death in the Northern Provinces. They cannot bear our birth struggle.

So I'm fatherless now, my darling, and he, out of whose seed I am come (though all these are mere words now, no substance left to touch), is gone. Neither wind nor water touch him. It is our love that is left, utterly bereft, whirling. A dry wind of anguish. Knowing the last threads are loosed and father, he who was father, has no need of us any more.

Mother is confined to her bed and will see no one. I do not even know where Mara is. Tomorrow, the feast of the dead. I hear the pots clatter. Axes bite into the flesh of the banana tree.

Wajida Tabassum

Hand-Me-Downs

"Oh no, Allah! I feel shy."

"Why should you feel shy. Haven't I taken off my clothes too?"

"Hm . . ." Chamki shrank back a little further.

"Are you going to take them off or should I call Anna bi?" yelled Shehzadi Pasha, whose veins coursed with the wish to command. With some trepidation, Chamki used her small hands to take off her kurta first, then her pajama . . . On Shehzadi Pasha's orders, she jumped into the soapy tub with her.

When they had both bathed Shehzadi Pasha turned to Chamki. With condescending fondness which had in it a large measure of possessive arrogance, she asked, "Now tell me, what clothes are you going to wear?"

"Clothes?" Chamki asked with great seriousness. "Just these—my blue kurta-pajamas."

"These?" Shehzadi Pasha shrieked and turned up her nose. "These filthy, stinking ones? Then what's the use of having bathed in water?"

Chamki asked a question in reply, "And what are you wearing, Pasha?"

"Me?" Shehzadi Pasha said with easy pride. "You know at the time of my bismillah my grandmother had an outfit with chanak chanak stitched for me. But why did you ask?"

Chamki was lost in thought, then she laughed, "I was thinking. . . ."

"What?" Shehzadi Pasha asked in some surprise. Just then they heard Anna bi shout, "No, Pasha! You chased me out of the bathroom, now why are you chattering with this no-good fool? Hurry up, or else I'll tell Bi Pasha right now."

Chamki spoke quickly, "Pasha! I was thinking that if you and I exchange our clothes and become odhni badal* sisters, then I could also wear your clothes, no?"

---

*Friends so close that, like sisters, they can exchange and share each other's clothes.

"My clothes? You mean all those clothes that are lying in my trunks?"

Chamki nodded uncertainly. Shehzadi Pasha was doubled up with laughter, "Ao, what a foolish girl. You know you are a servant—you wear *my* discarded things. And all your life you'll wear my hand-me-downs."

Then, with infinite love which held more arrogance than any other feeling, Shehzadi Pasha tossed the dress that she had shed for the bath toward Chamki. "Here, wear this. I have any number of other clothes."

Chamki was incensed. "Why should I? You wear *my* dress," she said pointing to her soiled clothes.

Shehzadi Pasha hissed angrily, "Anna bi, *Anna* bi . . ."

Anna bi rattled the door, which flew open since it wasn't really shut. "Oh, so both the madams are still standing around naked." She put her finger on her nose and spoke in mock anger.

Shehzadi Pasha immediately took down a soft pink towel and wrapped it around herself. Chamki stood as before. Anna bi glared at her daughter.

"And why did you take a dip in Pasha's bathtub?"

"Shehzadi Pasha told me to bathe with her." Anna bi looked around furtively to make sure nobody else was there, then she hurriedly pulled Chamki out of the tub and said, "Get to the servants' rooms . . . quick . . . you might catch a chill." Chamki shrank back a little self-consciously. "Don't wear these filthy clothes now. There is a kurta-pajama in the red box which Shehzadi Pasha gave you the other day. Put that on."

As she stood there, the little seven-year-old thought deeply and said haltingly, "Ammavi, if Shehzadi Pasha and I are the same age, then why didn't she wear what I took off?"

"Just you wait, I'll go and tell Maina that Chamki said this to me . . ."

Alarmed, Anna bi picked up Pasha and said soothingly, "You know, Pasha, this whore has gone crazy. Why should you tell your Maina about her ranting? Don't play with her, don't even speak to her. Just be silent and spit on her name, okay?"

Anna bi dressed Shehzadi Pasha, combed and plaited her hair, served her food, and, when she was done with all her chores, she reached her own room to find Chamki still standing unclothed, as naked as the day she was born. Without missing a heartbeat she began slapping her daughter. "You'll pick fights with those who feed you, you forward old hag! Now if the bada sarkar throws us out, where will we go, eh? Such a temper!"

According to Anna bi, it was a matter of great good fortune that she had been employed as a wet nurse for Shehzadi Pasha. Her diet was as rich and fastidiously chosen as any begum's because, after all, she suckled the only daughter of the Nawab Sahib. She got lots of clothes, too, because it was imperative that the wet nurse stay absolutely clean. And the best part was that her own daughter got any number of Shehzadi Pasha's hand-me-downs. Getting clothes was usual but, quite often, silver ornaments and toys also came their way. And here was this girl—ever since she had started growing old enough to understand anything at all, her only fixation had been *why should I wear bi Pasha's rejects?* Sometimes she'd look at the mirror and wisely state, "Ammavi, I'm much prettier than bi Pasha, aren't I? *You* make her wear the clothes I discard."

Anna bi would admonish her all the time. After all the privileged have a lot of power. If somebody got the slightest hint that it was that damned Anna's daughter and not the real daughter of the house who uttered such things, they'd surely cut off their hair and noses and cast them out. As it is, the years of suckling were long past. It was the tradition among such households that the wet nurse was sent away only on her death. Even so, one could expect to be pardoned only for those faults that are pardonable. Not for this!

Anna bi twisted Chamki's ear and said, "I don't want to hear any more of this, I promise you. You are to wear bi Pasha's rejects all your life. Have you understood, you child of an ass?!"

The child of an ass stilled her tongue then but the lava continued to boil inside her.

When Shehzadi Pasha turned thirteen it was her first Namaz-e-Kaza. On the eighth day was her gulpashi. For this occasion her mother bought her such a gorgeous, glittering dress that your eyes could hardly stay fixed on it. It had pairs of golden bells sewed on so that whenever Pasha walked there was a sound of many anklets—*chunn bunn*. In keeping with tradition even this exquisite, expensive jora was given away. Anna bi gleefully gathered up all these gifts and took them to her room. There she found Chamki, who by now was wiser and more self-respecting than her years would suggest. She said unhappily, "Ammavi, it is one thing to take such gifts because we have little choice, but please don't feel so happy when you take them."

"Just think, beta," Anna bi whispered, "even if we were to sell this jora it would fetch not less than two hundred rupees. We're lucky to have found a place in such a house."

With enormous longing Chamki said, "Ammavi, I wish . . . My heart's desire is that I also give some of my old things to bi Pasha sometime."

Anna bi struck her forehead and wailed, "Now look, you're getting older—learn what is good for you. What will I do if anybody hears you say such things? Have pity on my old bones at least."

Seeing her mother weep, Chamki fell silent.

Maulvi Sahib began both bi Pasha and Chamki on their Koran Sharif lessons and the Urdu alphabet. Chamki showed much greater intelligence and interest than bi Pasha did. When both of them completed their first recital of the Koran, the senior Pasha bought Chamki a new set of clothes of ordinary material, as a mark of favor. Though Chamki later got bi Pasha's heavy set, she treasured her own clothes more than her life. She felt no hint of slight in them. A pale orange dress was much better than numerous glittering clothes.

Now that Shehzadi Pasha was as educated as was desirable, and was the right age, appropriately enough there was talk of her marriage. The house became a hub for goldsmiths, tailors, and traders. All Chamki could think about was that even on the day of the biggest celebration, the wedding, she would wear only those clothes which were her own, not somebody's rejects.

The senior Pasha was a woman of great virtue and compassion; she always considered the welfare of her servants as she did that of her own children. So she was just as concerned about Chamki's marriage as she was about Shehzadi Pasha's. Finally, after nagging Nawab Sahib, she found a suitable groom for Chamki, too. In the general hubbub of Shehzadi Pasha's wedding, Chamki's nikah could also be managed, she thought.

The day before Shehzadi Pasha's nikah, the house was packed with guests. A gaggle of girls made the whole place gay and noisy. Shehzadi Pasha sat among her friends with henna on her feet and said to Chamki, "When you go to your husband's house, I'll put henna on yours."

"Oh, God forbid!" said Anna bi fondly. "May your enemies only have to touch her feet. That you said such a thing is good enough. Just pray that the boy she marries turns out to be as good and kind as yours."

"But when is she getting married?" asked one of the young girls.

Shehzadi Pasha laughed the same arrogant laugh that she had as a child. "There will be so many of my used things that her dowry is as good as ready," she said.

Rejects, discards, used goods—it was as if a thousand needles pierced Chamki's heart. She swallowed her tears and lay quietly in her room. As the sun went down the girls picked up the dholak again. Songs loaded with double entendre were sung. The previous night had been a *ratjaga*—an all-night celebration, and there was to be one tonight as well. In the courtyard at the back, the cooks were cooking various delicacies on a battery of fires. From the house, it seemed like broad daylight in the middle of the night.

Chamki's tearful beauty appeared even more attractive in her pale orange outfit. This was one dress that could lift her from the depths of her inferiority to the very skies. These were nobody's old clothes. This new dress, made of new material, had come her way but once in her life. The rest of it had been spent wearing Shehzadi Pasha's old things. And because her trousseau also consisted of Shehzadi Pasha's clothes, she would have to use them for the rest of her life. *But bi Pasha, a daughter of Sayyads can be pushed only so far and no further—you'll see. You gave me one old thing after another. Now you'll see.*

She entered the house of the groom with a large plate of *malida*. The house was decorated with rows of lamps and bustled with as much gaiety as the bride's. After all, the wedding was to take place the next morning.

In the huge house and general confusion nobody took any notice of Chamki. After inquiring here and there she reached the groom's chambers. Tired after all the ceremonies of haldi and henna, the groom lay sprawled on his bed. As the curtain moved, he looked around and was transfixed.

A knee-length, pale orange kurta, tight pajamas stretched over rounded calves, a lightly embroidered, silver-dotted orange dupatta. Eyes which swam a little, soft, firm arms emerging from short sleeves, hair adorned with garlands of white flowers, and a dangerously attractive smile playing on her lips! None of this was new, but a man who has spent the past several nights fantasizing about a woman can be quite explosively susceptible, however respectable and well brought up he may be.

Night is an invitation to sin. Loneliness is what gives strength to transgression. Chamki looked at him in such a way that he felt his very bones turn brittle. She turned her face away with calculated swiftness. He stood up agitatedly and planted himself before her. Chamki sent him such a look from the corner of her eye that he felt he was going to pieces.

"Your name?" he swallowed.

"Chamki," and a lustrous smile lit up the moon-like loveliness of her face.

"How could you have had any other name? You shine so . . . you could only be Chamki." He put his hands on her shoulders with a tremor. His attitude was not that of the usual male who chats up girls to seduce them. His hands shook as he took hers and said, "What do you have in this plate?"

Chamki replied encouragingly, "I brought some malida for you. There was a ratjaga . . . at night." She cut him to the quick as she smiled with inviting slowness, "To sweeten your tongue."

"I don't want any malida to sweeten my tongue. I . . . we . . . yes . . ." and he brought his mouth close to hers for a taste of honey. Chamki gave herself up to his embrace. To rob him of his purity, to lose her own, to plunder all of them.

On the second day, the day of the bride's departure, Shehzadi Pasha went to give her bridal costume to her foster mother's daughter, according to the convention of the family. Chamki smiled and said, "Pasha, all my life I have lived with your used things, but now you, too . . ." She laughed like one possessed ". . . all your life something that I have used is for you . . ." Her manic laughter wouldn't stop.

Everyone thought the sorrow of parting from her childhood playmate had temporarily unhinged Chamki.

Translated from the original Urdu by Manisha Chaudhry

Binapani Mohanty

Lata

Somewhere around midnight, Lata left her home and disappeared. No one knew to where. It was the full moon night of Holi, with moonlight splashing over the entire village. The deities had finally been brought to the festival grounds after being carried from house to house. Revellers thronged the narrow village lanes. The children had rested a little in the evening and, refreshed, had gone off to the grounds in a spirit of joy. With hidden handfuls of colored powder they had smeared one another's face, for the day of Holi could never be the same as the day before. Just once a year, and so hard to get hold of; how it comes and goes in the twinkling of an eye! And if one did not want to possess it, it seemed as though everything piled up, the grime and dust of the year sat heavy on both body and mind. And it was as if Lata went on smiling, yet inside her the fears of years settled in like ghosts. So on a full moon, festive night like this one, Lata mingled with the crowds, leaving her house to watch the jatra after offering her customary worship.

In the evening she ate her fill of rice and water and fried greens. She had spread a mat on the narrow veranda, muttering that she was feeling sick. Her father had shouldered the village deity and left for a distant village that morning. And here in the house, no one, not even a crow or a koel, that she could talk to. When her sister-in-law, Mani, came to ask her over for a game of cards, Lata turned her down, saying she was unwell. Mani and the others had gone back. Someone had taunted her from the backyard gate: "Look at her! There she is, lying like a log but says she is ill. Such lies!" All of them burst into laughter and the wanton breeze wafted it away, who knows where. Still, Lata continued to lie flat on her back, staring blankly at the moon. The festivities of the village remained outside her, did not touch her at all. And no one needed to know the inner world she dwelt in, or where her thoughts lay, save herself.

The rhythms of the mridanga and cymbals reverberated throughout the village, and the crowds moved here and there with vermilion-smeared faces.

Around midnight, without a thought for the denizens of the dark—the jackals and dogs and evil spirits—Lata shut her front door and left, as though for the Holi festivities. And nobody came near her house, nor cared to inquire where she was.

The revelry lasted all night. At daybreak, each person went home to rest, exhausted. Who had the time to go anywhere, or inquire about another? Who cared to find out whether someone had eaten or slept or died even! Who would be interested in Lata's whereabouts? When Jagu Behera walked into his house, fatigued, on the afternoon of the next day, he turned livid with rage when he saw the lock on the front door. His shouts for Lata were loud enough to be heard in the neighboring houses, but only their echoes rebounded and struck frenziedly at his chest.

For wouldn't he be mad? He had sold five plots of his fertile paddy land to marry off his daughter. His son-in-law was as handsome as a raja's son and possessed enough land and property, with a lot of mortgaged gold belonging to others. But his daughter didn't live with him for more than a couple of months. Only she knew what had transpired between them. Lata was all skin and bone in a month. She answered no questions, facing everyone with a blank stare, as though she were seeing a human being for the first time. And Jagu thought: here he had brought his daughter up with such love and care; a little inconvenience at her in-laws', and she was in a state. She didn't have a mother who would understand her problems; as a father, what else could he do? He wasn't a prince who could override her in-laws!

The world was calm and peaceful when the latch on Jagu's front door rattled loudly one night. A thin drizzle fell, a blanket of ominous clouds lay low in the sky. Frogs croaked along the edges of the village pond. A slight chill had made Jagu cover himself from head to foot and go off to sleep. The sudden noise woke him. His queries as to who the caller was brought forth no answer. Telling himself that is was a spirit, he turned on his side and went back to sleep. After a time the chains rattled again. Annoyed, Jagu opened the door, then fell back into the darkness, startled out of his wits.

His voice came out faint, halting, through his initial shock, "Lata! You!" It wasn't hard to recognize his daughter in the dark—after all, she was his own flesh and blood.

Lata did not utter a word, but slipped past him quietly into the house. Nonplussed, Jagu asked, "Now, what? How are you here in the middle of the night? Did you have a fight with your husband and run away?"

Lata remained standing, leaning against the wall, her head bowed. It wasn't possible to look into her face. In sheer desperation Jagu Behera slumped to the floor. When he noticed that Lata was making for her room without a word, he began again in a voice full of pity, "Come, tell me the matter. Did your husband or in-laws strike you? Are you all right?"

Lata slunk inside quietly. Jagu was sure that his daughter's situation must be intolerable, but things would ease in time, he thought. He didn't have to go into it at this time of night. Had the girl had her evening meal or not? She had always been an obstinate sort. Jagu felt restless. He found her sitting on the narrow veranda and asked, "Will you eat something? There should be some rice left." Lata, her head between her knees, burst into sobs, her body racked with pain. She hadn't wept like this even on her wedding day. He bent down to wipe her tears with his rough shoulder-cloth, then fell silent. Time would reveal this grief she wasn't able to bear. Perhaps she was homesick, too. Morning would bring her husband or her father-in-law, Jagu told himself, and then he would give them both a piece of his mind!

But did that happen? Months passed by, became a year, and still no one came for Lata. Jagu found it impossible to get to the root of the matter, and why Lata had left her husband's house still remained a mystery. She continued to answer any questions put to her with blank stares. At times, tears welled in her eyes, her lips trembled, but she never spoke a word. Jagu was silent, too, when asked about his daughter. In exasperation he would say that his son-in-law had gone to Madras to look for a job, and when he got one he would come for Lata. But there was no news from anywhere. No one came to inquire. And strangely enough, Jagu Behera never thought of going to Lata's in-laws to find out what the matter was either. The meager amount of money he earned from his daily wages was just enough for one meal for the two of them. But could Jagu get angry with her? Sometimes he sulked but forgot his own misfortune when he looked at her face. And who could tell that she wouldn't kill herself? Or run away someplace? Jagu had no one else in this world. Whatever Lata might be, reckless or stubborn, she was his own, and he would suffer with her. That was why Jagu, whose habit it was to mutter to himself all the time, was struck dumb. Tales of all kinds made the rounds of the village after Lata's arrival, and she was the butt of much sarcasm. But Jagu remained locked in his own silence. Come dawn, he would leave for the fields and, at sunset, he would prostrate himself before the gods to show him a way out.

Ah, the girl should be there when he returned, with a bowlful of rice and the door held open. But no, she was probably playing cards in some neighbor's house like an unmarried girl! How long could he take this? His impetuous shouts of "Lata! Lata!" fell back emptily on his ears. He wandered around from house to house in the village and came back in despair. The doors remained shut, as they had been. Only the shadows spread across the fields.

Jagu Behera lay slumped against the veranda wall. He felt exhausted. He remained there all through the night; at daybreak, awakened by the calls of the pheasants and crows, he glanced at the front door: it was shut, as before.

Villagers affirm that Jagu Behera never regained his will to live. Whenever elders came to console him, his lips would quiver and tears would stream down his face, but no sound escaped his lips. Everyone agreed that it was the girl's evil nature that was responsible for his state. And Jagu Behera lay as he was, a lifeless form, for days before he gave up the world forever. But his eyes remained wide open, as though riveted to the front door.

Three years have passed since then. Three years since the day of Jagu Behera's death. In the festival grounds three annual fairs have been celebrated, mango trees have shed their fruit and blossomed again, the floodwaters of the river have battered the shores and mingled with the sea. In the meantime, Lata's cousin gave birth to a son and became a widow. Childhood friends scattered far and wide. Still, no one had any news of Lata. Why she had left home, and whether her husband had taken a second wife, no one seemed to know or care. But the sun continued on its daily rounds and the seasons came and went with unceasing regularity. Lata remained a forgotten entity, a useless question mark. From that day Jagu Behera's house stood shut, as though forever. A small, one-room house with a narrow veranda and, inside, just a tin trunk, a couple of reed mats, and some torn sheets. Everyone in the village knew of Jagu's belongings, but not even the poorest of the poor was tempted by any of them. Then again, who wasn't afraid of evil spirits in the dark, especially in an abandoned house? Even the jasmine shrub had stopped flowering. Slowly, the shuttered, silent house took on a haunted air, and, inexplicably, passersby seemed to hear the loud, drawn-out calls of Jagu Behera coming from its livid darkness.

All of a sudden, one day, there was an uproar. Three years had become three long centuries. Events of the past were now vague and unclear. Shouts of, "Save us! Save us, oh lord!" could be heard from people who knew nothing about the incident. For, early in the morning, Lata was seen sweeping the veranda of her hut, with a two-year-old child tagging behind, thumb in its tender mouth. A slight bulge had developed around Lata's waist, her body and face had grown fuller. Still, her two large eyes seemed to be on the brink of tears, as if she would break down at the slightest bruise. News of her return spread like wildfire: Had they heard? Jagu Behera's wayward daughter had come back! And with her was a child. Must be hers, or why would she have brought him along? One who could run away from a handsome husband in the middle of the night, would she have done that without reason? Age was creeping up on her steadily, and she had realized she couldn't earn her livelihood doing hard labor anymore. So here she was, back in her father's home.

And what a difference there was between the Lata of today and the girl of three years ago! She seemed so listless and lax. Just stood there, her head covered with her sari, when village elders questioned her! When the womenfolk of the neighborhood came along, she spread out her torn mat on the floor and stared at them. She kept silent, not reacting even to their playful taunts. Sometimes a smile would flit about her lips, or she would draw rice-powder designs on the earthen floor, unmindful of their stares.

Everyone accused her of being a harlot. Let her live the way she wanted to, they said. Who cared what she did? No one had ever seen someone who had abandoned her husband and then become a mother act as though she were an innocent! On top of everything, how arrogant she was! Was she some goddess that she could do whatever she pleased? Transform the unreal into the real so that she could live on with her dreams? What a shameless hussy! Couldn't she get hold of a little poison? Would she be able to live on if she just kept her mouth shut for all time?

Lata's meager knowledge, acquired from a few years in primary school, was hardly sufficient to show her a way out of her troubles. Nor did she have a father or a brother who could be a support to her. Finally the villagers came together and decided that Lata had to leave the village or else they would set Jagu's hut on fire. It was as though her actions had blackened everyone's faces, put their women to utter disgrace. She had to go.

When the villagers crowded around Lata's front door that evening and demanded that she explain her actions, she put the edge of her ragged sari between her teeth and said, "Yes, the child is mine. The day after our marriage, when my husband left for Calcutta, my in-laws locked me up in a room for fifteen days without food or drink; they didn't even look at me! Somehow I escaped in the middle of the night, back home to my father . . . but father was so distressed the days I was here; he heard no end of people's taunts. And I—I was the butt of much scorn. I can't forget how he labored day and night to feed me in his old age, yet our hunger remained, the disgrace never left us."

Lata swallowed, pulled the edge of her sari down onto her face and went on, "And I had nothing to tell people, nothing to do. Even death shunned me. I couldn't free my father from his unending labors. Then this cruel world left me with a son and flung me back here."

From somewhere in the group, a middle-aged man suddenly tightened the washcloth around his waist and took two steps forward. Lata didn't know who he was. She heard him shout, "What did you say? Tell us again! The world gave you a son, and you couldn't leave him somewhere else but had to bring him here! Ha! These tight-lipped ones have the sharpest tongues! Go ahead, tell us, whose son is this?"

Lata hid her face with her sari and sat down, trembling, on the ground. The child's eyes filled with tears which began flowing down his cheeks; sobs racked him, but no sound escaped his lips.

Suddenly a kick landed on Lata's waist. It was the old mother-in-law of a distant cousin of hers. As she broke into tears, the old woman screamed, "You bitch! Is there a frog stuck in your throat that you cannot speak? Haven't hurt a fly ever, have you? Yet you weren't able to live with your in-laws, you swallowed your own father alive! And now you have the cheek to say this is your son, gifted to you by mother earth! Confess who the father is! Or else I'll be the one to cut you in two. Don't you know me?"

The old woman's foot quivered on the poor girl's flesh. Men and women gathered around, enjoying the scene being enacted before their eyes.

Lata's neck twisted and sagged, lower and lower. Her sobs were choking her. Suddenly sparks began to fly from her eyes. It was impossible for her to bear it anymore. The earth wouldn't open up to swallow her even if she wished. Only if she wished, would she live, or, if she wished, die.

She'd settle things herself.

Whatever happened then, happened suddenly and quickly. Lata flung off the old woman's foot and stood up. Her face was a mixture of courage and hate, and it was turning a livid purple. Her gaze, stern and full of purpose, swept over the crowd, from one end to the other. With the child whimpering in the crook of her waist, she began.

"So you want to know who the father is? Here, before you, are all his fathers! Ramu, Bira, Gopi, Maguni and Naria—maybe three or four others! How can I say who the father is? It was the night of the Holi festival, the revelries were at their height and suddenly from nowhere, Ramu was throwing his washcloth across my face as he lifted me forcibly into the dark. Beside the funeral ground, under the bushes, they crowded around and picked the flesh clean off my bones. My mouth was gagged. But it was easy for me to recognize their faces in the clear moonlight . . . How can I tell who the father is? Ask the low-caste Haria who escorted me to Cuttack—all for a few rupees! And just to spare my father the indignity, I didn't come back. Even then I kept my mouth shut. But now *you* ask them, Aunty! Let them place their hands on their chests and tell you truthfully who the father is!"

The whole atmosphere changed. The old and middle-aged exchanged glances, the young gave knowing smiles. No question was asked and none was answered. Meanwhile the old woman had flopped down on the veranda, as though spent. Ramu, Bira, Gopi, Maguni, and Naria kept their eyes on the ground.

Lata wiped her tears and began sweeping the veranda. The child started yelling, without reason. Lata flung the broom down, cleaned the snot from the child's nose and picked him up. She cuddled him close and mumbled, "Why do you cry, my child? Ah, my pet, I am here with you. Don't you worry. Who's there man enough in the world to admit he's your father? There, there, your mother will take care of you."

What the boy understood only he knew, for he flew up into the clouds. He stretched his arms toward the moon and broke into spontaneous laughter. Its sound startled the bystanders, and they started to disperse slowly, their heads lowered.

The few jasmines that had blossomed on the bare tree appeared to smile in the breeze. Lata's neighbor, the slanderous old woman, leaned on her stick and hobbled away in silence.

Lata looked around her and spat on the child's tiny chest to ward off the evil eye. Her handsome son had seemed to wither under their gazes! She would take care of him. She owned the plot of land that had been her father's, and her son would be its master one day!

The earth and sky, as on other days, were still, motionless. And Lata was smiling and weeping at the same time.

Translated from the original Oriya by Jayanta Mahapatra

Rajee Seth

Against Myself

For the last ten days Shyam has been like one possessed. He will not sit still even for a moment—Donations! I need donations! Devji is dying in the hospital. Without care!

Tearing around, he tries to piece together for me the strands of Devji's disjointed life: "Did you know that he has been living away from his wife since his youth? No small achievement, to live without a wife at that age, and it isn't as if he was carrying on with someone else. And why did he leave her? You probably think there was some basic discord. None! Just for a principle. His creativity! And you probably want to know why that is the woman's fault. But do you understand? When a larger principle is at stake, then one can't worry about smaller issues. If he hadn't lived this way, would he have been such a great writer? Never!"

He paces restlessly, his voice rising slowly. But his anxiety isn't disturbing, simply because I know so well how excitable he is. Whatever he thinks, he thinks so passionately!

At this moment, the inert body of Devji lying in a hospital bed is the hub of Shyam's attention. He collects funds round the clock. Pleads with everyone. Whether they can afford it or not! I wonder how much of his drive is marked by Devji, the writer, and how much simply by his own obsessive self?

His efforts were fruitful. Devji came round after ten days of semiconsciousness. Whether his creativity will survive this shock to his nervous system remains to be seen, but for Shyam this is a major victory. Even though he is crushed with fatigue. Being caught between the hospital and the funds-race has drained his face of all life. I have never seen him so wan!

And my compassion for Shyam would have flowed unchecked had he not said, "I cannot see a writer waste away, Ruchi! I just can't."

"But you've been doing just that for so long!" The words rushed to my lips and stopped just there. Instead I mumbled indifferently, "You are so good to others!" I could see that he needs his rest.

Everything would have stayed calm if only he hadn't spoken that one sentence. Calm, but at a cost! But that is another matter!

He was so tired he slept instantly, but for me that whole night . . . it was like being torn apart soundlessly on the edge of a blade.

When I married Shyam he was a budding journalist. Fond of writing, vibrant, outgoing, and obsessed with the need to pare down everything and reach its core. Even if sometimes this curiosity cost him a great deal. But since the sheer act of undoing something was like destroying it, where then was the core? If only he had been a little reflective he could have been a good writer.

When I met him, he was brimming with the promise of a writer. He had that germ of creativity. But an individual journey is decided by so much else. Yet I was so certain of his talent and believed that journalism was merely his prologue.

In those early days, when he had given me his eagerly woven, touching little verses, I was entranced and slowly began to lose myself in him. And that slow enticement I found so inevitable!

After the wedding I had spent an entire day at my mother's, collecting my diaries, letters, incomplete literary writings, and my favorite books. All safely packed in a bag. It was imperative for me to take all of these along. At home, there had been something lacking in my life despite the warmth of my parents' love. A fragile dream caught in the folds of my soul—me lying on Shyam's chest, my hair spread out, reading out poems from pages which flutter maddeningly . . . reading my verse to Shyam and mesmerizing him. He would be so overwhelmed by it, and then there would be between us the verve of competition, the enthusiasm and the rapport. . . .

Those wonderful days in the valleys of Simla after the wedding! Only women, perhaps, can be so stupid as to start toasting their literary dreams on the warmth of a love that is just kindling. But when some lines of poesy strumming up in my mind made it to my lips, Shyam promptly sealed them there. Instead he let loose a trail of fire on my body.

In the cold, misty dawn, light trembled upon those mountains, carrying with it the distant snowy peaks right into the window of our hotel room.

Splendor unleashed! An almost speechless wonder, and then something would begin to stir in the womb of my mind. And the hovering lines of poesy would suddenly crystallize, urgent to be set to some inner rhythm.

But before they could form, Shyam would pull me back into his arms. And it would start again: that journey of exchanging one kind of bliss for another! But . . . when the mind is consumed with a specific joy, nothing else will quite do . . . a silly feminine dilemma!

After that came all those beginnings—a new house, friends, furnishings, relatives, and responsibilities. The kind that happen everyday, to everyone, but don't really have a name and are never noticed.

In this nameless monotony, whenever I retreated into my precious world, I would open up my bag of papers, read each line, repeat each page, and Shyam would agree that he was not the only one who could write good poetry!

"Why do I need to write anymore? There is no goddess who needs my offerings now," he would say.

He lauded my work generously and he wasn't an ordinary critic. But his praise stoked hope once again. This would be another path to win his love, draw him to myself! This was no longer the way-to-a-man's-heart-is-through-his-stomach age! And Shyam was a journalist! There is a thin line between journalism and creativity. The footsteps taken in both can be heard on either side. And Shyam has that creative seed . . .

One day I sent off a story to a magazine. I wanted to surprise Shyam. The story was returned after fifteen days. I was so disappointed that I couldn't keep it from him. When he saw the editor's note he was strangely terse: "If you had wanted to send it why didn't you tell me? What do you understand of the commercial world? You think talent is enough!"

Even though my dreams lay frozen somewhere, there seemed to be a sliver of hope under the ice. How stupid of me! I am the wife of such a renowned journalist and I didn't ask him for help! Even if I only had wanted to surprise him! Whatever Shyam touches will be covered with gold dust! And he is mine, my husband!

My imagination was on fire once again. I began to toil. After lunch when Shyam went back to the office I would sit down to write. By the time he returned I had not always tied up all the ends. I was pensive, inexplicably lost, lines dogging my mind, and chattering on about just that one subject.

"Who said that I am a fan of Shakespeare or Tagore?" he said sharply, suddenly one day.

"Why, must I know you all over again?" He didn't smile at my dig but turned grim.

"Your mind is captive. It is by you, for you, just you!"

"We are both captive. It is the same cell and we are imprisoned in the same interest," I reasoned as I put my head on his chest, but he embraced me with such violence that . . .

What should I have called that emotion, I wondered for a long time after!

I was like an addict. The long days now resounded with the music of poetry. I was going mad. Shyam! You too must experience this joy! The thrill of creativity. And because you know it, you must share it. You! My partner! And see, a creative trance can turn even your name into music, tender, traditional, and yet so new!

At night I egged him, childlike, "Shyam, let's see if you can get these two poems published."

"Why, is it such a great challenge?" he said, stroking my lips with his fingers.

"But you accept it, don't you?"

"No!" his voice was curt and harsh. I was unnerved. This was not a joke anymore. It was an unambiguous rejection and free of the strain of any justification.

"Why not?"

He did not answer.

"Tell me, why not?"

"What should I tell you? I just said it. We will see."

And I chose to see merely fatigue and work pressure in his response.

"And you worried about something?"

"No! Come and sleep near me."

And his embrace was untouched by ire, tension, or the sharpness of his mood. It was effusive as always!

"I'm not going with you to the club today," I said when he was almost ready.

"Why?" he turned as he knotted his tie.

"I don't feel like it! I'm in a different mood. Why don't we stay at home?"

"And I'm supposed to bask in the shadow of this other mood and smoke opium!"

His sarcasm was biting and unexpected. "Shyam!" I shot back, equally sharply, and went into the kitchen.

He didn't go to the club either but took off his clothes and lay down to read a magazine.

"It would have been better if you had gone to the club alone," I said, returning to the room.

He did not answer. That moment had already been shattered.

There had been no direct reference to my writing still, but small comments were slowly linking up around it. One day I gathered courage and asked, "Shyam, could it be that you don't like my writing?"

He was incensed. "You are crazy! How can I be against writing? I was once a writer, now I live in the world of writers. I even understand quality and here you are accusing me of something so preposterous!"

"Well then . . ." my voice broke.

"Well nothing! You are suspicious without reason."

"It is not a suspicion. If it were, then why should it cast such a shadow on my soul?"

"Yes, but false premises also create shadows. That's what you are suffering from."

"Perhaps," I conceded. I, too, was not sure now. I gave him the benefit of the doubt and said, "I must have erred in understanding you."

"Of course!" he would grow magnanimous again. Take me in his arms and the whispers in my ears would allay all doubt.

My poems were piling up. The lines and pages filled an entire notebook. I felt as if it were all being written with my blood. In the second reading I was reading through Shyam's eyes. In the third round I would see his face beaming with pride and praise, and by the fourth . . . I felt like running to him with my little treasure!

But . . . some unnamed part of me had seemed to have died and I could never quite make it to him. I could never pinpoint a moment of receptivity in his happy, genial, loving self.

A joy which cannot be shared slowly dries up in exclusion.

One day he spotted my book. Leafed through it. He stopped and read some bits too.

"You have written so much. There is so much of you outside me. I didn't even know!"

"You don't want to know. Every day I wait for you to want it."

"But I want to know everything about you."

"That's a lie! If you had wanted to know me, would you have ignored my soul to this degree? What is created is an integral part of one's self."

"I know," he sat down, looking shattered. What is it that suddenly crushes him? There is just no bond between my creativity and his being, and yet . . .

And I suddenly knew that the writer was dying in me. Without reassurance, without support. Today what he says he cannot see happening to Devji, has been happening in front of him, to me. To the creator in me, starving to flower and dying piecemeal. Doesn't he see how he has broken me this way, so much that . . .

One day when he came home he saw the small flame in the courtyard. "What are you burning? Old love letters?" he chuckled.

I was seething. "Don't jest," I snapped.

"Come inside, then I can do something else," he teased and tried to drag me inside.

I stood rooted to the spot. He kept holding on to my arm. Suddenly he jumped as a piece of my notebook sparked away from the flame: "What is this? Your book of poems!"

I looked at him—this was it! The moment of punishing him and freeing myself from my agony.

He was shocked. His shoulders sagged. "What have you done, Ruchi? You don't know what you have done!"

"I did what you wanted me to do. For you! You always wanted to push me this far and break me into pieces."

"Oh God!" he sat down on the floor, his head between his hands. I watched in silence. Then he stood up, gently held me by the arm, and took me into the bedroom. There he dropped his head in my lap and burst into tears.

Watching him suffer felt good. His anguish also convinced me of the importance of my work. But somewhere I also knew that I had wanted to punish him but had punished myself instead. It was all a fistful of ash now, yet why, in that moment, did I find it easy to forgive?

"Will you stop crying and say something?" I said gently.

"No! No!" something was tearing him up inside. "You have . . ." he could barely speak, "you have insulted me, you have . . ."

"Speak up! I can't understand you, Shyam."

"You won't understand. I couldn't bear to see you . . . this split in you . . . I couldn't bear . . . and for that you gave me such a cruel punishment."

Something hardened inside me. He did not like my being split into pieces, but he was the one who had divided me thus. He had cut me into two by not accepting one part of me. One, secure for himself, and the other, left to rot within me! What he really wanted was to possess me. Totally! But for that he would have to accept me as a whole first. Did he even know that?

Caressing the head lying on my breast, I felt that I should hand him the weight of my resentment. Explain to him once and for all the truth behind the split.

But he wasn't really waiting for an answer. He was babbling away, "I don't want to love anything more than you and neither can I bear to think that you should love anything more than me."

I don't know what happened to me then. I somehow couldn't gather the nerve to freeze that moment, his overpowering emotion . . . perhaps I never will. I kept thinking that I will say it some other time. Knowing all along that I never will! He wants me to give of myself. All. To him. Demands the right to possess me. His natural right. And whenever I try to explain to him while I caress his head on my shoulder, explain to him the inevitability of my two parts, then I will be at war with myself. Against myself! Demanding back my share in our oneness and keeping it back for myself. Just myself. Alone!

I have never been able to gather that courage even today. Even though every hour I see the promise in my soul grow slowly barren, hear it banging its head and calling at my closed doors.

Translated from the original Hindi by Jasjit Purewal

K. Saraswathi Amma

The Subordinate

Paru Amma sat motionless, unaware of what was happening around her. The boiling rice overflowed and put out the kitchen fire. On her right hung a screen made of coconut fronds. Sitting there, she could see, through a hole in the screen, everything that took place in the house opposite, which was situated on higher ground. She knew all the details of that house—the number of rooms, the location of the kitchen, the layout of the bathroom, et cetera. Whenever anyone came to live in it, Paru Amma couldn't help reminiscing about her own adolescence. Then, the memories of the house engulfed her.

Today there was a great deal of noise and activity going on there. The commissioner in charge of temples had arrived with his two daughters and they were staying there. The various preparatory jobs intended to please the boss were assigned to subordinate workers. The job given to Paru Amma, the sweeper of the temple, was . . .

She shivered with fear as she dwelled on the events of the morning.

For the past two days Paru Amma had been suffering from an attack of arthritis, so Lakshmikutty, her daughter, was sent to do her work at the temple instead. This morning Paru Amma woke up from her sleep only at ten. She was sitting in the eastern veranda, soaking in the morning sun and rubbing her swollen left knee, when the assistant from the temple arrived. He stood in the courtyard and boldly stated his business.

For a long time Paru Amma did not utter a word. The request was made on behalf of the commissioner, her boss. If she did not comply with it . . . Her thoughts did not dwell on the justice or injustice of the request. Nor did the assistant reveal to her that this was his own ploy to earn the special appreciation of the commissioner.

Noting Paru Amma's silence, the assistant said, "Just this one time, allow it. Serving the boss, is it so insignificant? His driver told me that there had been no difficulty in organizing these things wherever the boss went.

So, think of the consequences before you raise any objections and create problems. Someone may point out to him that it was you who objected. You may not have the strength to bear the consequences of his displeasure."

Paru Amma said in a slightly raised voice, "If Lakshmikutty had been your sister . . ."

"Keep quiet!" In a voice reflecting his wounded self-esteem, he said haughtily, "How can you compare that fatherless child to my sister?"

The question put an end to Paru Amma's half-stated reproach. The assistant thought she was weakening in her resolve and added in a conciliatory tone, "I will arrange to send Lakshmikutty back soon. After the worship of lamps at twilight, the boss will leave his daughters in the temple and return alone to the house. At that time I will come here personally and take her to him. If you raise your voice or show any sign of protest . . ."

Then, in order to prevent her from seeking some other escape route, he threatened, "If the boss wants he can easily cook up a police case against you. Your daughter's plight will then be truly miserable. All of us will be taken to task. This is a better solution. It will be good for your future, too."

Paru Amma realized that her words would have no effect, so she kept quiet. The assistant left, feeling that everything had been settled to his satisfaction.

After that, Paru Amma did not have a moment's peace. She knew she had to stay calm and think of a way out. But how was it possible to think and plan on this day of Krishnashtami* when her thoughts were neither cool nor collected? She had kept herself alive for years in anticipation of this one day in a year, Krishnashtami.

For Paru Amma, the Ashtami Rohini day in the month of Chingam marked the celebration of the anniversary of an event that had taken place when she was seventeen years old.

In the days when this village did not have a snake doctor, Krishna Pillai came here with his skills to cure snake poisoning. Since he had both talent and luck, he acquired quite a good name. The drawing teacher of the local school made a board with a rectangular piece of wood, drew the figure of a snake with its raised hood in the left-hand corner, inscribed the words, "Treatment for snake bite will be done here," and hung it in front of the snake doctor's house. It was, in effect, a certificate given by the locals in recognition of the doctor's skills.

At home also, he was lucky to have a good woman as his wife. But,

---

*Lord Krishna is said to have been born on the eighth day (ashtami) of the month of Chingam, the first month of the Malayalam calendar. His birth star is Rohini, and his birthday is known either as Krishnashtami or Ashtami Rohini in Kerala.

unfortunately, she died prematurely, leaving behind a three-year-old daughter, her anguished husband, and the locals in misery.

The doctor took a second wife who earned the nickname "Serpent" from the locals. The doctor himself felt that she personified all the venom that he extracted from his snakebitten patients. Under her reign, his once peaceful house was transformed into a hive of quarrels, beatings, loud crying, and fasting. The doctor could feel the presence of poisonous fumes lurking all over his home, and whenever he thought of his little daughter he felt a searing pain within.

Harassed by the tyranny of her stepmother, Parukutty was convinced that it was neither her parents' karma nor her own work ethic that would decide the happiness or sadness of her life. She felt that it was nothing but a living hell, yet did not contemplate either suicide or escape from it. In the beginning, she would wither under the scorching flame of her stepmother's anger, but gradually she learned to remain emotionally unmoved by any cruelty meted out to her.

Much later, she learned even to endure the pain of momentary pleasures—they gave her the strength to live.

Five or six years after her father's death, her stepmother bought a piece of land opposite their own home and began to construct a new house there. She was assisted by her brother in this venture, and soon he began living with them as well. Now Parukutty's sufferings increased. When the building was complete, it was rented out to a munsif and his family.

It was Parukutty's seventeenth birthday. Yet on that day she did not get anything to eat. By the evening she was weak with hunger; she sat on the parapet of the western veranda of the house and began to weep, thinking of her father.

"Look here, look here!" On the compound wall of the next house stood three or four children, calling out to her. She looked up and saw their grandmother standing behind them. "Don't cry, come over here," she said kindly. "I'll give you whatever you need."

Later events proved that the old woman truly gave her all that she needed. There were other needs she craved—love, tenderness—needs which nurture both body and soul, and these, too, were fulfilled from the same quarter. Anyone else in her place would have wondered whether the aftereffects of such a complete fulfillment were altogether desirable, but does anyone, gripped by hunger, refrain from eating food laced with poison even though death is inevitable?

The inmates of the "other" house were the munsif; his wife; their three children; the munsif's brother, who was a lawyer; their mother; and two or three servants. The mother of that house had grown up in a family of more modest means. Later she became affluent on account of her husband's luck and status in life, but was always kind to poor people, especially those who had once been rich, but had fallen on hard times.

Parukutty's main job was to look after the children of the house. Once in a while she would wash the clothes and sweep the floor. The one job she loved was collecting flowers for the morning and evening pujas performed by the mother. During the day she stayed in that house; at night, in her own home, she slept on a bed made up of the cruel words of her stepmother and her stepmother's brother. Both of them had much to say about her working in a neighbor's house and besmirching the family name, but Parukutty's heart, enveloped in the sweet memories of the day, was impervious to their hurtful, piercing words.

Thus was a light kindled in her otherwise darkened life.

All of a sudden, the munsif received transfer orders. He left for his new workplace with his wife, children, and servants, but the lawyer-brother, who was now earning well, decided to stay on.

It was then that the mother decided she needed only Parukutty to look after her son and herself. Their day-to-day requirements, left in the hands of a young and grateful Parukutty, were managed with greater efficiency and dignity than before.

On an Ashtami Rohini day in the month of Chingam, at twilight, the lawyer came back from his office, had his evening tea, and set out for his walk. He was attracted by Parukutty, who was approaching from the opposite direction. Parukutty had worn her hair loose, caught in a knot at the end. She wore a clean white mundu and a light blue blouse and held a plate filled with different flowers—hibiscus, sankupushpam, antimandaram, basil, jasmine, and pavizhamalli.* She had the innocence, youth, and untouched beauty of a guileless seventeen-year-old girl.

The lawyer and she faced each other in the middle of the staircase. She bowed her head and tried to ease her way out by keeping to one side of the stairs. Some inner compulsion made him ask inanely, "Where is Mother?" She stopped, turned to him, and replied, "Mother is having a bath." He climbed up two steps, looked at the plate and asked, "Why have you collected so many flowers today? Is there any special festival?" Now she raised

*Local Kerala flowers. The sankupushpam, blue in color and conch shaped, has sexual connotations. The pavizhamalli is a small, white flower with a coral stem. Tradition has it that Lord Krishna's two wives, Rukmini and Satyabhama, would fight over who got the flower from Krishna. It is commonly grown in Kerala homes, even though it symbolizes discord.

her head and looked directly at him. "Don't you know that today is Ashtami Rohini? Mother might think that even these are not enough for the puja."

He stood rooted to the spot, attracted by the fragrance of the flowers and the beauty of the girl who held them. "Do you know who you should worship on Ashtami Rohini day?" Parukutty was taken aback by her young master's words and the expression on his face. But she was suffused with a rare kind of inner happiness and said, "I know. Today is Lord Krishna's birthday. I have plucked all these flowers for his worship."

Gopalan Nair moved closer to her. "Then do that. I am also named after Lord Krishna. Worship me. I, too, love flowers."

Parukutty stood there in amazement, unable to move. What did he mean? If his mother were to see all this . . . She said hastily, "Please take whichever flower you like. It is time to prepare for the puja."

"I deal only with stacks of paper, how would I know the value of flowers?" Her bemused expression pleased him. "You pick a good flower for me."

Parukutty's fervent wish was to escape from there somehow before his mother saw them together, although her youthful ardor may have wished otherwise. She picked out some jasmine and pavizhamalli flowers and gave them to him. "Please take these." He stretched out his hands—not to take the flowers, but to hold the hand that extended them to him. Parukutty was anxious, but at the same time an inexplicable joy filled her being. The plate slipped from her hand and fell to the ground. When he heard his mother's footsteps in the distance, he said, "Mother is coming. Pick up the flowers and go to the puja room."

As it was Ashtami Rohini, the puja lasted longer than usual. Until now, whenever Parukutty entered the puja room she would feel the presence of Lord Krishna and, in her mind's eye, see only the form of that divine cowherd with his flute. But today, however hard she tried, she saw only the figure of the man who smiled at her and said that he, too, had the name of the Lord. She folded her hands, which today had felt a man's touch for the first time, and then prostrated herself in front of the Lord's idol. Her fervent prayer was, "Lord, help him to grow into a great man. May I be of help to him, not a hindrance."

It was as though Lord Krishna heard her prayers and granted her wishes—but in a totally unexpected manner. Before the next day dawned, the mother had to leave in a hurry—a telegram arrived from the munsif to say that his child was seriously ill and urgently required his mother's presence.

As soon as she was ready to leave, she called Parukutty to her and said, "I am not sure when I will return. Please look after Gopi till I come back, and see that he eats his food on time. He doesn't usually like food made by anyone else, but I think he likes you. After the day's work is done, give him his supper, then eat yours, and go back home. That way, no one can point a finger at you. Please do whatever you can to make him happy."

Whatever she may have meant by this last instruction, Parukutty obeyed her meal-giver's words to the letter. She fulfilled all Gopalan Nair's desires in a spirit of self-sacrifice. The result of that fulfillment—yes, there was an inevitable result—she bore alone. She had no companion, nor did she wish for one.

When the mother did not return as promised, Parukutty was panic-stricken. She was afraid that she might become an obstacle in this man's path, a man destined to be the husband of a rich and lucky girl who would help him attain a respected and honorable position in life. She was even more worried about creating a wedge between the mother, her kind guardian, and her favorite son, thus earning a reputation for ingratitude. Even in the midst of passionate lovemaking, her common sense prevailed, and she knew instinctively that, in real life, love scenes enacted in the secrecy of the dressing room could seldom be the prologue to scenes of marriage. She consoled herself with the thought that she would at least be filled with memories of happy times with her lover, even after his departure.

No one suspected the true nature of their relationship, and life went on as usual. In front of strangers they behaved like master and servant, distant from each other; at other times, they were true lovers, united in their love. But this dream life did not last long. One day Gopalan Nair called Parukutty and asked, "What will you do when I leave?" The question unsettled her. She remained quiet for a while and then said, "I will work and earn a living."

"You mean you'll do the same work you did for me, for the men who come to live here after I leave?"

Parukutty looked hard at him. She understood the innuendo and her eyes blazed in protest. Mastering the self-respect of a poor but proud woman, she retorted angrily, "Those who wish to do an honest job will always find one. No one in my family has resorted to prostitution to earn a living."

This answer from a young girl who was not even eighteen stunned the lawyer. His selfish ego was satisfied with her resolve to remain faithful to him even after he left. He said lovingly, "I will arrange for a job for you which will give you your livelihood—the job of a sweeper in the temple of Krishna. I have just to mention this to the Commissioner of the Religious Board, even ask my mother to recommend your case. The bride chosen for me by my brother and mother is the commissioner's daughter. You'll receive your appointment order even before my marriage. I'll give you some money for your expenses till the order arrives."

Thus Gopalan Nair bade farewell to the village and to his legal profession. Parukutty, who was not in the habit of worrying about problems that can never be solved, wept copiously. When it was time for him to go, her heart was overwhelmed with gratitude and love, and her eyes filled with tears. Gopalan Nair tenderly wiped them away and departed, his own eyes brimming.

Within a month, it became clear to Parukutty that Gopalan Nair had kept his promise, and in about four months his generosity became evident in another form as well. "My daughter has looked after that lawyer so well that she has already become a mother." Her stepmother's cutting remarks continued, but Parukutty remained indifferent. She loved her child not only as part of her own living spirit, but as a memorial to an experience she could never forget.

After that, eighteen Ashtami Rohini days came and went, reviving old memories in Parukutty's heart. With each new year she would forget the all-important Tiruvonam* and remember only Krishnashtami. On that sacred day, at twilight, when the worship of lights began, the devotees who thronged the temple would assail the Lord with their personal problems. Among them stood a poor idealistic woman, her thin hands folded in prayer, completely unaware of her material existence, reciting a totally selfless prayer. In fact, it was her only prayer. May the Great Lord be kind and give the creator of her illegitimate child all mortal happiness while he was alive, and heavenly peace when he died.

This morning, too, Paru Amma's prayer for her lover was uppermost in her thoughts. But the unexpected arrival of the boss's assistant upset her tranquility.

Paru Amma couldn't understand many things: why should her daughter be subjected to such an experience in the very house that had stood witness to her own days of love? And that, too, on the anniversary of her first initiation. Was it some sort of punishment from the Lord?

Paru Amma remembered how a beautiful new world had opened up for her, unexpectedly. But it was soon closed and locked up by the owner himself, who proceeded on his life's journey, taking the keys with him. Still, she had her memories. What would happen to her daughter? The scandal might cool off with the changing winds of time, but to lose her virginity for a man, any man—even if he be an emperor—for a day's pleasure. It would

*The day King Mahabali was banished to the netherworld by Vamana, an incarnation of Lord Vishnu. In Kerala, people celebrate Onam in memory of the good times they had during King Mahabali's reign.

leave her no sweet memories of love, nor yield a relationship that would blot out every other.

Paru Amma saw before her a life bleeding constantly from painful memories—memories that would be erased only after death.

Suddenly, a new thought scorched her mind—a thought totally alien to her motherhood. She saw a vision of her daughter's body—bleeding, throbbing—but it lasted only for a moment. After the deed was done, where would she seek shelter? Would a murder go unpunished? Those servants of death with red caps, manacled hands, the prison cell, the judge's den—filled with eloquent lawyers. Many such images flitted across Paru Amma's mind's eye. But her stepmother had trained her to look upon any suffering as insignificant.

Lakshmikutty had a bath and left her long hair loose, caught up at the end in a knot. She came and stood in front of her mother with a plate full of flowers. She shook her by the shoulders, trying to wake her from her day-dreaming. "Mother, I finished sweeping the temple premises before I had a bath. The assistant told me that I need not go to the temple again. Mother, the commissioner and his two daughters came to the temple. We have never seen girls like them. They wore glittering saris, skirts, and jewelry. A sight to dazzle the eyes! The assistant asked me to put some flowers in their hair. Just imagine! I stood near the commissioner and put the flowers in their hair. But they do not resemble their father."

Paru Amma looked at her daughter unblinkingly. She understood why the assistant had made Lakshmikutty perform that task. She could imagine the whole scene as though it had taken place in front of her. Poor girl! How could she know the helplessness of being born a woman in a poor family! Paru Amma said, "Go and string the flowers into a garland quickly. It is time to light the lamp."

Lakshmikutty left to carry out her mother's instructions without changing out of her wet clothes. Paru Amma took off the rice without checking whether it was properly boiled, placed it in a coir hanger, and went across, through the western side, to the house opposite.

In the temple, it was time for the worship with lamps. In the opposite house two well-dressed girls were putting the final touches to their attire. They were lucky. As Lakshmikutty had observed, they were the prototypes of their mother. Lakshmikutty's creator, too, could have been the owner of such a prosperous household. Lakshmikutty's creator! Paru Amma faced the temple, closed her eyes, and joined her hands in salutation. Then she placed the memories of days gone by as an offering at the feet of the idol.

Lakshmikutty leaned against the wall coated with cow dung and began decorating the idol of Lord Krishna. The sound of a conch reverberated from the temple, making Lakshmikutty's heart surge with worshipful love.

Paru Amma stood behind her daughter, with hands joined in prayer, and watched her performing the rituals. She could not concentrate on the worship at all. Hearing the sound of a footstep, she turned. She knew it was the assistant even though she couldn't see his bulky figure properly. Lakshmikutty, who was bending to place a garland on a picture of Lord Krishna, fell down with a half-formed cry of agony.

In a few moments, the courtyard of that small house was filled with people.

Paru Amma who stood in front of the Lord, eyes shut and hands folded, heard nothing. Her thoughts were concentrated on the Lord, born to protect the helpless and reestablish dharma. Even her daughter's bleeding corpse did not distract her. She cast back in time to that Ashtami Rohini day, eighteen years ago, and remembered the man who bore the name of the Lord.

"Commissioner! Commissioner!" The crowds whispered and parted on both sides. The visitor asked in an authoritative voice, "What has happened?" His voice drew Paru Amma out of her deep meditation. She turned her head and looked at him. The commissioner bent down, taking care not to hit his head on the low ceiling, and stepped into the veranda. A gas lamp was placed beside him. People inwardly praised his compassion that had brought him to this poor house to find out what had happened. He pointed to the blood-drenched corpse on the floor and asked, "Who did this?"

He caught the hint of a smile on her lips.

Paru Amma prostrated herself before the Lord's photograph, then turned to face him. She noticed that he was no longer lean and handsome but fat and ugly. She said in a neutral voice, "I did."

"Why?"

"Death and prison are preferable to wayward living."

Her tone and attitude moved him. He suspected that in some way she held him responsible for this cruel deed. Without revealing his distress, he asked, "What is the relationship between you two?"

How dare she smile, forgetting her subordinate position! She said, "This is my daughter. Nearly twenty years ago a woman lived in that house for some time. She was called Lakshmikutty Amma. I have given my daughter her name in memory of my devotion to that family."

The commissioner's mind raced back to the days of his youth. From among the many thousands of blurred images of women he knew, the figure of a seventeen-year-old girl emerged clearly. Parukutty, who had succumbed to his desire without any fear of humiliation. After he left her, for a few days her figure had come before his mind's eye unexpectedly, but slowly it had blurred and disappeared.

The commissioner looked carefully at the woman in front of him. He must be wrong. Her long, lustrous hair, could it have been reduced to this measly cock's tail? Could that face have become so ugly? What could have happened to the ruddy good health and physical beauty of that girl who had stood in front of him and proudly declared her fidelity?

Suddenly his eye fell on the girl whose body was covered in blood. That mother's health and beauty—had it been poured into another being created and generously donated to her by him? He shuddered with revulsion. If his guess was correct, then that girl pointed out to him by the assistant in the evening, what was she to him?

His voice shook a little, but he covered it up hastily, assuming an air of officiousness and asking, "What is your name?"

Paru Amma bent to rub her swollen knee. Then she said calmly, "My name is Paru Amma. Earlier, everyone used to call me Parukutty. Now people will recognize me only if you refer to me as Paru Amma, the sweeper of the temple."

Translated from the original Malayalam by Vasanthi Sankaranarayanan

Ajeet Cour

Dead End

The darkness outside was thick and opaque. Only the howling of dogs ripped across the dark shroud of the night.

I was unable to sleep.

Ever since my brother Kewal was murdered, sleep had eluded both of us—me and my mother, who was numb with grief. But we both pretended that we were sleeping, so that the other should keep her eyes closed. Sleep sometimes just saunters into closed eyes, they say.

They think my brother was killed by extremists. I have no idea. He hadn't hurt anybody. Why should anyone kill him?

But the murderers could be anyone. Extremists, or anybody else. How long does it take to kill a human being anyway?

It takes months in the mother's womb to make a human form. It takes years to then bring him up. The living being who takes the longest to grow is the human child. And then, just one metal bullet! In a fraction of a second, everything is over. Like a full-blown balloon pierced with the tip of a pin.

Walking on two legs, breathing, the heart singing rhythmically inside the rib cage, and he is called a human being. Just pierce him with one bullet, and the blood spurts out. What is left is a dead body. Just a handful of dust! Everybody waits impatiently to take the body to the crematorium. "It is just mitti, a handful of dust. Send it to its destination. Why delay?" That's what everybody said.

It happened just four weeks ago. But I feel as if centuries have gone by.

I don't feel like getting up when the sparrows start singing in the morning. How can they still sing? I wonder.

Both of us would like to continue with the pretense of sleeping. Getting up forces you into a meaningless routine. We don't feel like cooking, but I force myself to cook so that my mother pushes a morsel or two down. She does the same, to make me eat. We pretend to eat so that the other eats, too.

Sometimes I wonder about the killers. It is quite possible that Sarla's brothers killed him. They had threatened to. Not once, many times. Sarla? Didn't I tell you my brother was in love with her! She was his classmate in that college in the city where he was studying. Sarla's parents and brothers thought Kewal had no right to be friendly with their Brahman daughter. Yes, they are Brahmans, and Kewal was the son of a low-caste Kamboh family.

I could never understand how Kambohs were low caste, because their traditional occupation used to be dyeing clothes. How can the people who make ordinary, drab-looking clothes come alive with rainbow colors be low caste? For that matter, how can people who create beauty by weaving cloth, by dyeing it, by stitching it; by transforming hard, foul-smelling dead hides into beautiful footwear and bags; by molding ordinary clay into beautiful pots and pans, be low caste?

Our forefathers were dyers. But my grandfather had departed from the traditional occupation; he was a schoolteacher. And my father was an employee in the postal department. He was very keen to give both Kewal and me a higher education. He always told us, "Nobody is born high or low. All these divisions of caste and religion are man-made. They might have been useful at a certain point of time, but they have lost their relevance today. It is only one's deeds and achievements and human values which make one high or low."

When I told this to my friends, they smiled condescendingly. And my classmates who were outside our intimate circle didn't hesitate to say openly, "All the low-caste people say that. They just try to fool themselves. But they can't fool the others."

I never thought much about these things. Life was so full of books, and love, and all the newly discovered secrets of life and living, that I never wasted my thoughts or time on these irrelevant things. My father was the best father in the world, my mother was affectionate and warm, my brother and I were on the same wavelength, and I was lucky that I was studying in high school. That was enough for me. But ever since Kewal has been murdered, all this keeps buzzing in my head. I don't think of them. They don't occur to me in any clear sequence. They are not even in clear focus. They just keep buzzing inside my skull which seems hollow after so much crying. I can't cry anymore.

Our father had told us that one of our forefathers used to dye Maharaja Ranjit Singh's turbans. The Maharaja was so happy with their vibrant colors that he gave him a large jagir, a few acres of land. That is how the following generations drifted into farming. But the family kept multiplying, and the land kept getting divided. My uncles were still farming their land, while my grandfather had given his over to a sharecropper. That sharecropper's family was still on our lands and gave us our fair share of wheat and rice, and lentils and vegetables, which was a great help, of course, because my father's salary was not enough to see us through school and then college.

I was in the final year of school when our father passed away. Kewal was in the first year of his graduation. He wanted to leave off studying and take up a job, but my mother said, "No, you must fulfill your father's dream." So he continued. Since there was no local college, I had nothing to do after school except wait for Kewal every evening, when he came home and taught me whatever he had learned during the day.

We were very close.

And now he is no more. My life is a yawning abyss, and so is my mother's.

Why do people have to go on living even after they lose the will and desire to live?

That night I had a strange premonition, as if a horrible danger were hovering over my head. These days I often get this feeling. A meaningless, nameless fear grips me. Two bloodthirsty eyes of a carnivorous animal glare at me from the darkness around.

What sort of danger can it be? Danger was a living, throbbing presence while Kewal was alive. Every morning, both my mother and I struggled with the lumps in our throats when he left for college in the city nearby. It was only when he came home safe in the evening that the lumps dissolved.

But now that Kewal is gone, what danger can threaten us? It has lost all its teeth, and relevance, even. There is no greater danger than death, and death has already visited this house.

Hearing the howling of dogs in the distance, I felt as if they were directing their lament toward our house alone.

I got up and walked on tiptoe through the three rooms of the house. On my knees, I peered under the cots. Only the shadows of the cots were discernible in the faint light of the lone diya flickering in front of Kewal's portrait. These shadows had a sinister presence, and I felt they were turning on their bellies. I felt terrified, though the refrain, "What danger? There can't be any more dangers. They have already killed Kewal. What else can happen?" kept humming in my head.

I came out into the back courtyard. In a corner, from the watertap, drops of water kept falling at regular intervals on the cemented patch where we clean the utensils and wash our clothes. In the eerie silence, even a tiny drop of water can sound deafening.

Darkness can produce magical horrors. The brass pitcher lying in a corner looked like a man sitting on his haunches, with his head between his knees. There could be someone hidden in the bucket even, or under the haystack, or behind the pile of firewood.

At the far end of the courtyard, near the back door which opens onto the back street, there was a small room in which we kept all the useless stuff, and also the wheat and potatoes and onions that our sharecroppers gave us after every harvest. There were a number of old trunks, too, in which quilts and durries and khes were stuffed, and also lots of old clothes that nobody ever used.

I hated these old, colorless wooden and tin boxes because they smelled of bygone ages and dead ancestors. But at this unearthly hour, during which people slept and grappled with their nightmares and dogs kept a vigil and wailed, a few grief-torn people, like my mother and I, wandered like lost souls in the twilight zone between life and death, between sleep and wakefulness. People like us are neither alive nor dead, because both life and death are decisive, and all decisiveness had evaded us.

We were not even waiting, the way all sad people wait: for a better tomorrow, for the wheel of fate to turn, for a ray of bright sunshine, for life! For us, everything was over.

Without thinking, I pushed open the door of this back room and peered in. It was dark. I switched on the light. A zero-power bulb came to life. I was a bit surprised because I was almost sure that the bulb would have fused long back. Nobody ever came to this room at night, except when some unexpected guests dropped in and we needed extra bedding. It was ages since anyone came here to stay; not since my father's death.

Moving listlessly in the room, I was thinking of all these guestless years, when I got a rude shock, like touching a naked electric wire.

I saw his eyes first. They looked like the eyes of a wounded deer whose neck is caught in the powerful jaws of a tiger. Both death and fear of death were frozen in those eyes.

After the first rude shock, I realized that his eyes were very innocent.

I tried to relate those eyes to his face. Every muscle in it was tense with terror. Even his short, curly beard was trembling with fear.

He was terrified of me, and I was afraid of him. Both of us were unable to move.

I felt my legs shaking under me. Who was he? How did he come to our house? What was he doing here? What did he want from us? Did he want to kill us? The way the others had killed Kewal!

And then I realized that he was clutching his leg with both hands, with blood oozing out of a small, red, raw wound.

He whimpered, "Water . . ."

He was wounded and he was begging for water—only these two facts registered for me clearly. Nothing else mattered.

I went to the kitchen and brought back a glass of water. My hand was probably shaking when he almost snatched the glass from me. Was I still afraid of him? I don't know. Perhaps I was, even though I knew that he was at my mercy.

He gulped the water down in one go. I could hear the sound of gurgling in his throat. He emptied the glass and stretched his hand toward me. I again went to the kitchen, refilled it, and took it back to him. This time he drank slowly, and kept the half-emptied glass beside him.

He looked at me. Now he was a little relaxed. The naked terror in his eyes had receded, and a black stillness had taken over. A few purple dots of (perhaps) anger were floating in those two black pools of silence. But the anger was evidently not for me. He was angry at his own helplessness, at the open wound from which blood was still flowing.

"Don't be afraid, sister, I'll go out silently as soon as I am able to move. Don't worry."

He spoke, and the mountain of ice between us began to thaw. The lump of terror in my throat also softened. The throbbing fear in my ribs was calmed.

I again went to the kitchen and filled a glass of milk from the karhai that my mother always kept on the slowly dying embers and hot ashes of cow dung cakes, throughout the night. He sipped it slowly, looked at me softly, and said, "Do you have a piece of cloth to tie this wound with?"

I opened an old wooden box, took out Ma's old dupatta, and handed it over to him. He wrapped it around the wound and tried to tie the edges into a knot. His hands were trembling. I sat beside him, caught hold of the edges, and tied them into a double knot.

"It's a bullet wound," he said softly.

"Bullet?" I shuddered.

"Yes, bullet. Those police dogs . . ."

"Police?" I was frightened again.

"No, don't misunderstand me, please. I am not a thief. Nor a smuggler. I . . ."

"An extremist?" I tried to keep my voice from shaking, but the effort was beyond me.

"Extremist? Is it a special species, bibi?" he smiled.

Suddenly his face contorted, his teeth clenched, and his jaws jammed. I could see dark pain in his eyes. He clutched his leg, just above the wound, and doubled up over it.

I was feeling helpless.

"Go and sleep, bibi. Let the pain subside a little, and I'll leave."

"You won't go anywhere." I suddenly felt responsible for him. I almost ordered him, "You won't leave in this condition."

I got up, locked the room from outside, came back to my cot and lay down.

I was sharply aware of all the sounds in the street. The night was passing too slowly, like a frightened black cat on its padded toes.

After a long, long time I felt daybreak approaching. Almost terrified by the daylight that would soon crawl in, I got up and rushed to the backyard. I filled a small lota with water and unlocked his room. I heard him moaning softly, without making a sound, as if a shaft of solid air was slicing through the stillness in the room.

I said softly, "Day is about to break. How will you then go out for your . . .? Well, here's some water. Try to get up and I'll take you outside. Near the outer wall. I'll stand guard. Nobody passes this way at this hour."

He bent over with pain as he got up. I held his arm, undid the bolt of the back door, and pointed to a place in the shadow of the wall outside. I kept the water jar near him and, with my back toward him, I spread out my veil like a protective tent.

I was like a hen, protecting her helpless, wingless chick, because the black kites and eagles were hovering in the sky above, searching for their prey with bloodthirsty eyes. I felt like a mother protecting her wounded son. A flood of tenderness heaved gently in my breasts.

I heard the splash of water and then he got up, holding the wall with one hand. I helped him get in, bolted the door, took him back to the room, and made him sit behind the boxes. I took out a quilt, folded it and kept it under his wounded leg. I gave him two pillows, and a khes to cover himself with.

In the morning two policemen came to our house. It was not unusual. Ever since Kewal had been murdered, police kept coming to our place on routine investigative rounds. But that day, seeing those two in police uniform, I panicked.

They said, "Last night there was a minor encounter between a police patrol and a group of extremists. Just on the outskirts of this village. You must have heard the firing."

Yes, we had. But these days the sound of firing is nothing unusual. It is a part of the usual sounds of the night—cicadas and frogs and dogs.

They said, "We suspect it was the same gang that murdered Kewal. Nobody was killed in the cross fire. They escaped under cover of darkness. But we are sure that at least one of them was injured. We could clearly see the trail of blood leading into the village. He must be hiding somewhere. You shouldn't worry. We will nab him soon and unearth the mystery of Kewal's murder, too. We won't let the bastard escape."

"In fact the trail of blood enters this very street and then . . ." said the other. "But you shouldn't worry. Just keep the house properly bolted from inside. We're going to search each and every house."

The words were like a thunderclap in my ears. Like a whirlwind they engulfed me, and I stood motionless near the door. I could hear the great, thunderous footfalls of my blood racing through my veins.

It was midday. The sun was like an angry eye looking down on the earth. With my mother moving from one room to the other, I couldn't go to the room at the back. Ever since Kewal's death my mother has taken to roaming around aimlessly, as if she has lost something; she can't remember what, but has to find it, nevertheless.

After eating, my mother sat down on her cot and opened the Gita in her lap. I knew the words would keep floating around, getting lost in the air, and she would keep seeing Kewal on the open page before her.

I had made four extra rotis for the boy in the back room. I put some cooked brinjals and potatoes on the rotis, covered them with my chunni, and took them to him.

He looked younger in the daylight. He was lying there, with his head on the pillows, his eyes closed. His face looked innocent and helpless, contorted with pain. His beard was a mere splash of light brown hair, short and curly. I was sure that, under the curly hair, there would be a dimple in the middle of his chin.

I touched his elbow softly. He opened his eyes. Black pain floated in them. His eyelids were a little swollen and red. Perhaps he had been crying in the darkness last night. He was hardly eighteen. Thinking of him crying didn't surprise me.

I extended my hand with the rotis toward him. He said, "I'm not hungry." He held his wounded leg with both hands, tried to extend it and get up, but collapsed with pain.

"You have to eat even if you're not hungry," I almost ordered him, the way you do small children.

He held the rotis and started eating like an obedient child. I looked at the glass, it was empty. I went to the kitchen and brought him water.

He was eating silently. I saw that the cloth with which I had wrapped his wound last night was soaked with black blood. On either side of the "bandage," I could see his leg swollen and red.

"It must be hurting like hell," I said softly.

My tenderness touched him. His eyes were moist when he looked at me and said, "Yes, the bullet is still inside."

I shuddered. An ugly bullet, made of solid metal, concealed in the soft flesh of the leg, poisoning the blood! It was a strange feeling, visualizing this horror.

He needed medical treatment. But what sort of times were we living in, when getting medical help risked exposure to death!

For him, all the doctors and surgeons had become irrelevant because their instruments had rusted with the curse of these times.

I came out of the room and locked it.

In the backyard the afternoon sun slumbered. I walked across and entered the room where my mother was still looking at the open pages of the Gita. I took out a soiled fifty rupee note from the small basket in which my mother kept needles and threads, covered my head with my chunni, and came out into the street.

I looked around, from one end of the street to the other. On the left, outside the grocery shop, three policemen sat on a long bench, engrossed in gossip.

I started walking the other way, came out of the street, and walked to the chemist's shop. This chemist used to be quite friendly with my father, the way people living in small villages usually are with one another. I said, "Chachaji, I need a packet of cotton-wool and a bottle of Dettol, and some gauze too." Though my voice was hoarse, I tried my best to sound natural.

The chemist, whom all of us called "Doctor," asked with concern, "Is everything all right? I hope bharjaiji hasn't hurt herself?"

Everybody was particularly concerned about us after Kewal's death.

I said, "No, nothing particular. She just didn't see the grinding stone and knocked her foot against it."

"Should I come home and bandage her foot?" he asked.

"No, it's nothing, really. I can do it myself. Don't worry, Uncle," my voice shook as I said this.

He looked at me from behind his eyeglasses, and quietly handed over the bottle of Dettol, a packet of cotton-wool, and rolls of bandages.

How will I carry all this? I wondered, thinking of those three policemen sitting outside the grocer's shop in my street.

"Do you have a carrier bag, Uncle?" I asked hesitantly.

He took out a plastic bag and stuffed everything into it.

I carried the bag to a grocer's shop nearby, bought a packet of salt and put it neatly over the other things, and walked back home.

The three policemen were still there, gossiping.

My mother had dozed off. I went to the room in the back courtyard and unlocked it. He was moaning, bundled up with pain. I removed the dupatta from his wound. It was an ugly, blackish gash, swollen, with clots of blood encircling it. I soaked the cotton-wool in Dettol, and, as I cleaned it, I was painfully aware of a similar wound that I had seen on Kewal's back, which didn't need any cleaning because he was already dead.

A black whirlwind was moving in mad circles inside my head. I was trying to push it back with all the force of my will power. In my ears I could hear the buzz and beating of my own blood, but I was trying not to listen to its mad fury.

He was biting his lips, trying not to scream. When I kept a large pad of cotton-wool soaked in the antiseptic lotion on his wound and wrapped a bandage around it, I could see a thousand black furrows of pain on his face. He was holding his leg in a firm grip with both hands, and his eyes were moist with tears of anguish that he was trying to hold back.

I felt like pulling his head onto my shoulder, patting it, and saying softly to him, "Cry my child, cry. Cry out your pain. Don't push your tears back because they freeze inside, and become big rocks weighing your soul down."

But I didn't. I couldn't say anything.

I went to the kitchen and brought him a glass of hot milk. I locked the room from outside and washed my hands with soap to remove the pungent odor of Dettol, but it lingered on in my pores.

I went to the kitchen and prepared tea. Took one glass to my mother, sat on my cot with the other one, and started sipping.

I was oblivious to my surroundings. Only that black swollen wound floated before my eyes, and, sometimes, those three policemen gossiping out there in the street.

I don't know when I lay down and went to sleep.

Even in sleep, a part of me was wide awake, listening to any sound that might signal danger. I was keenly aware of the threat lurking around, ready to pounce on him whose name I didn't know.

In my fitful sleep I saw vast deserts, frightened rabbits running for their lives, and ferocious dogs chasing them, snarling, howling, panting, with their bare white teeth flashing, and their red tongues hanging from their black jaws.

It was the howling of dogs that made me get up with a start. I was soaked in cold sweat, frightened. Evening shadows were lurking ominously in the corners of the room. Mother was not on her cot, and outside in the dark there was the sound of barking somewhere in the distance.

I got up and came to the backyard. Mother had lighted the fire in the kitchen and was looking at the leaping flames with her chin on her knees. There was a pan on the chula in which dal was being cooked.

She sat there, unaware of me, unaware of the pan on the fire, lost in thought, deep down in the black well of her pain.

And then she looked at me, trying to focus her thoughts, and said slowly, "Do you have a headache? You slept for so long. It isn't good to sleep in the evening, when day and night meet."

What worse could happen? I wondered.

Silently, I looked toward the locked room at the back and said to my mother, "You should rest now. I'll make the rotis."

Ma pressed her knees with her hands, sighed, got up, and went out.

After serving my mother, I kept four rotis in a thali, put some dal in a bowl, poured piping hot butter on the dal, and took it to his room.

He was probably sleeping, with his mouth slightly open, like a child. I touched his arm—it was burning hot. I put the thali down and touched his forehead. It was scorching hot, and moist.

He didn't open his eyes. Every breath of his was a soft moan. I looked at his leg. The swelling had increased. Black blood had oozed out of the bandages.

In dejected helplessness I came out and locked the door again.

I couldn't eat.

At midnight I again went to him. Opened the door and switched on the light. He was doubled up, bent over his leg. His helpless moans were heartrending. I touched his head. He didn't look at me.

The food was lying in the thali, untouched. A white layer of butter covered the dal.

I lifted his head and forced him to take some water. I don't know if he was aware of my presence or not, but he did gulp down a little water, and again bent over his leg.

Behind the old wooden and tin boxes that contained age-old abracadabra, he looked like a bundle of soiled clothes. And outside all those people were looking for him.

Next day he was delirious with fever. Almost unconscious. He only took a few sips of water whenever I managed to go to him, lifted his head, and touched his lips to the glass.

It was evening and his fever was blazing. I soaked a towel with cold water and kept it on his head. A strange smell emanated from his wound. I changed his bandage.

With the cold, wet towel on his forehead, he opened his eyes. I gave him some hot milk. He sipped it slowly, and then said, almost in a whisper,

"I don't want to die here. If I do, how would you take my body out? Bhain, I have already been such a great bother. I don't want to put you to any more trouble."

I felt like crying. I placed my hand on his head, the way mothers bless their young ones when they go to school for the first time. And came out.

I looked around. Where could I sit and pour out all the pain flooding my soul?

Just then, there was a loud knock on the outer door, the door that opens onto the main street. I was startled. My mother asked irritably, "Who can it be at this unearthly hour? They should know there are two lonely women here."

I went and opened the door. Outside stood the same two policemen who had come the previous morning. They said politely, "Bibi, we know we needn't search your house, but every time our dogs sniff the drops of blood, they stop here. Can we take a look inside?"

I was terrified. Real, naked terror was churning inside my belly. I said, "Ma has just dozed off after eating her food. You know she hardly sleeps. If you can . . . if . . . after an hour or so . . . perhaps?"

"Don't worry. Let Maji sleep. We'll come back after an hour. There is no hurry. But we hope you won't mind our coming in at night."

"No, it doesn't matter. You are like my brothers. You have been looking after us since Kewal's death," I said softly.

They left.

"Who was it?" asked Ma.

"Some policemen. Wanted to search this house. They are looking for someone, and they think he is hidden in one of the houses in this street."

"Have you bolted the door properly?" asked Ma anxiously. I assured her I had and she lay back on her cot.

On tiptoe I walked to the back room.

Perhaps he had also heard the knock at the outer door. How could he, in the condition he was in? I can't understand even today.

He was awake. His face was alert and his eyes full of terror.

"Who was it?" he asked.

"Policemen. Wanted to search the house. They'll come back after an hour." I wanted to off-load my entire burden. He had to know. The moment had finally arrived when he should know.

He made up his mind suddenly. How can one arrive at such decisions in a fraction of a second? A decision that would probably catapult him straight into the jaws of death!

"I must leave," he said, and staggered up.

I didn't ask him to stay. I couldn't. Both of us knew that we had reached a dead end, that all roads were blocked, that there was no escape now.

The danger lurking outside for the last two days was about to cross the threshold and enter.

His face contorted with pain when he tried to take a step forward. With clenched teeth biting into his lips, staggering, he took another step. And then another. And stepped out of the room.

I opened the back door. Stepping out into the street, he halted for a moment, a very brief moment, and looked at me. So many different emotions were mingled in the dark pools of his eyes: affection, gratitude, and also the shadow of death. There was so much more, too, for which I can't find any words. Human language hasn't yet found words for all those other emotions floating in the dark pools of those eyes.

I only know that his eyes, and all those silent emotions in them, will follow me around as long as I live. They will keep haunting me, always. They will come and nestle close to me in all the silent moments of my life.

He went out. I bolted the door from inside and stood there, rooted, trying to hear the silent sound of his departing footsteps, trying to smell the danger in the air.

Suddenly the dogs barked. Many of them. They were barking in a mad fury. And then the sound of bullets pierced the stillness of the night outside, and blew my soul to shreds.

I am telling you the truth. Believe me. I didn't hear his cry. I only heard the sound of bullets, loud enough to rip the earth open. But no human cry.

I could also hear many heavy shoes running up and down the street.

Ma was probably in that azure zone of half-slumber when the body sleeps but all the senses remain awake and alert. Perhaps she was seeing Kewal in her dream, floating in the twilight no-man's-land between sleep and wakefulness.

She heard the sound of bullets and got up. Abruptly. In a frenzy she rushed toward the front door, opened it with a thud, and ran barefoot into the dark street outside, crying in a heart-piercing wail, "Don't kill. Don't kill him. Don't kill my Kewal. Don't kill my little one. Don't fire at my dove, don't fire at him! He is my only son, my Kewal!"

With her arms raised, her dupatta trailing behind her, her hair disheveled, she ran barefoot on the naked bricks of the street, begging, imploring the darkness, "Don't kill him! Don't kill my little one!"

Translated from the original Punjabi by the author

Chudamani Raghavan

Counting the Flowers

"Brinda! Bring the coffee, child." Brinda brought the coffee.

"This is Brinda." Take a good look, the tone of his voice added.

And the visitors did. The girl was not fair skinned, only wheat colored. But a wheat colored vision! Her face and figure vied for supremacy. Of more than average height, she had a luminous air of easy, natural grace about her that brushed aside poverty as one might shake off a fly.

"Prostrate before visitors." It was another command from the girl's father. Brinda prostrated before the visitors.

"Sit down, child," said the boy's father. Brinda sat down and fixed her eyes on the nagalinga tree visible through the window in front of her.

The boy's mother glared at her husband. Was it not for *her* to invite the girl to sit down? And the girl, too, had sat down at once. Really!

"Please drink your coffee," the girl's father urged, doing the honors.

"Oh, yes!" The boy's mother turned to the girl, "How far have you been educated?"

The girl's father gave a start. Had the marriage broker not apprised the bridegroom's party of these details?

"We had to stop her schooling with the Eighth Standard."

"Not good at studies, I suppose?"

Brinda looked intently at the tree. On top, at a great height, the dense green foliage fanned out against the sky. Clusters of thin offshoots sprouting from the lower branches hung down, heavy with flowers. Flowers resembling serpents' heads, each with a lingam inside, as if crying out to be christened nagalinga. Petals of pink and pale yellow all around. In the center, the snake's raised hood over the tiny knob of the lingam. These flowers certainly had a beauty all of their own.

"Actually, she was very good at her studies and wanted to continue, but we didn't have the facility."

"Why talk of facility? Schooling is free."

"I meant the circumstances at home. My wife does not keep well. And I am often away on duty, being a traveling medical salesman. So Brinda had to give up school and stay home to look after her mother and the family, and run the house."

"It does not matter," said the boy. "Going to school isn't all that important."

This was totally unexpected. All eyes, except Brinda's, turned toward him. His mother's face went red with anger. Even his father gave him an embarrassed look that plainly bemoaned his naiveté, as he said, "Isn't it surprising for a girl not to have completed her school education these days, when even a B.A. is so common?"

The girl's father voiced his anxiety, "I had asked the broker to tell you everything about us. Didn't he do so?"

"Oh yes, he did."

Then why the questions, the girl's mother seemed to ask silently as she raised her head for the first time to look at the boy's mother. Just for the pleasure of saying, "Not good at studies?"

"Your coffee is getting cold," said the girl's father. The visitors drained their tumblers.

"Good coffee," commented the boy's father, mentally adding that these people must have prepared it specially for this day.

"Brinda made it. The bondas and sojji were also made by her. A very competent girl, our Brinda. Adept at all household arts." The girl's father spoke with the pride of a salesman advertising his wares. The girl's mother sat with her eyes carefully averted from her daughter, afraid that she might break down if she looked at her.

My, my, how many flowers there were on that tree! Brinda counted them as far as her eyes could reach. One, two, three, four, five . . . Before she had counted up to a dozen, the flowers got mixed up. Had she counted the one on the upper branch or not? She guessed that there would be about three dozen flowers in all. A wealth of delicately hued blossoms, silken in their softness. There must be many more strewn at the foot of the tree. The strip of wall below the window obstructed the view. She would be able to see better if she stood up.

"Why is the girl so quiet?" asked the boy's mother and turned to Brinda with the question. "What are you looking at so intently out there?"

"At the nagalinga tree," Brinda said without lifting her gaze.

"What's the idea? Turn round and talk to us."

"Talk about what?" Brinda's eyes had still not budged from the tree. Suddenly she began to talk. "Do you know about this tree? It has its autumn at least four times a year. For days on end you see it shedding its brown leaves in the wind. They pile up thick and high on the ground. You have a tough time sweeping out the place. And then, in just a few days, right in front of your eyes, the green leaves appear again, fast and fresh, and cover the entire tree in no time! You wouldn't believe it was the same tree that had been bare such a short while ago. Even as the dead leaves are falling off, the tiny new green ones are sprouting alongside—what an enchanting sight! Almost as if the old tree has sloughed off its skin and a new one was appearing from within."

The boy was looking happily at the girl, a fact noted both by his mother and the girl's father.

His mother seethed inwardly. Did the wretched boy have no pride, for God's sake? His eyes were going to pop right out of his head . . . She controlled her temper and, wanting to distract him, turned back hastily to the girl to say, "Your father said you made the tiffin. Can you cook meals also?"

No, there were not three dozen flowers. Perhaps four or five short. The petals were spread out wide and had created the illusion of there being many more than there actually were. Nothing more.

"Brinda, didn't you hear Aunty?" rebuked her father. "Why don't you speak? Turn round and answer her."

Brinda turned toward the lady, "What did you say, Aunty?"

"I wanted to know if you can cook."

"I can."

"What did I tell you! Our Brinda is very capable," said Brinda's father.

"Hm."

"The eldest of our sons, Seenu, is also a capable, brilliant boy. If put through college he will do very well and come up in life. Perhaps you would consider helping us with this . . ." The girl's father smiled ingratiatingly, remembering what the marriage broker had advised: "There's no harm in your asking them, anyway."

The boy's parents took some time to get over their shock. Then: "Well, I like that!" the boy's mother exploded. "We have been generous enough in making a concession to your circumstances and agreeing to accept only ten thousand rupees from you for the marriage, including dowry and everything, and now you want us to educate your son as well! Has anyone heard the like of this?"

"Calm down," the boy's father said to his wife. "Let him ask what he likes. We are not going to agree, after all. He is only expressing a wish."

"Wish? But this is greed! One doesn't shoot off one's mouth like that . . ."

"I didn't say anything improper, madam," said the girl's father. "I was only asking for help. And it is not as though we are going to be strangers to you, we'll become your kinsmen through this marriage . . ."

"There are many parents who demand even half a lakh of rupees from the bride's family, while we made you a concession by settling for only ten thousand. Did you think of that? No! And on top of it you have the gall to make this outrageous proposal!"

"That ten thousand is fifty thousand for us, madam! We are poor people, as you know. Yet we incur this expense because we do not wish to deny our girl entirely. If you will only think of that and be kind enough to help us with our son . . ."

"You are only doing your duty for your daughter. How are you justified in making that an excuse to profit from us? If you get back all your money's worth from us like this, what do we have left—we, the bridegroom's people?"

Brinda began to look at the nagalinga tree again.

"Don't you have anything left?" asked the girl's father. "What about the girl herself? And such a girl, too!"

"Uneducated," said the boy's mother. "You ought to give us three thousand rupees more for that reason alone."

"But what about her efficient household work? You should cut down a couple of thousand for *that*."

"Efficient, my foot! The bondas were too hot. The coffee smelled of raw powder. What is a marriage without the boy's people getting at least twenty thousand rupees? But we, in our broadmindedness, have agreed to a mere . . ."

"A beautiful girl is worth more than twenty thousand rupees."

"That's a laugh. What effrontery! It was only because the broker had said the girl wasn't too bad-looking that we agreed to this small sum. Normally a boy's parents would expect not less than thirty thousand rupees . . ."

The girl's father glanced at the boy. "For *this* boy?" He did not voice the question, but the boy flushed and instantly pulled in his right leg under his dhoti. His parents, too, fell abruptly silent.

The girl's father chuckled softly, "Why should we bandy these arguments? The broker has informed both our parties of how matters stand, hasn't he?"

"Then let us finalize things. Why bring up a new issue like your son's education?" asked the boy's father.

"That isn't such an objectionable suggestion . . ."

"Has anyone heard of the boy's people educating the girl's brother? It is just not done. What game are you playing, mister?"

"The broker happened to mention that quite a few earlier marriage proposals for your son have fallen through," the girl's father said in a smooth voice.

The boy's father mopped the beads of perspiration that broke out on his brow. The boy's mother paused a while, then said, "All right. Make it fifteen thousand and we'll help with your son's education."

"If I were that well-off, wouldn't I help him myself?"

"Then forget it."

"Wouldn't you like to earn credit for educating a deserving poor boy? After all I am giving you a good-looking girl and ten thousand rupees. Just a small favor in return . . ."

"Do you want this marriage to come through or not?"

Sensing their anger, the girl's mother's eyes lit up for a moment in sudden hope. She made bold to turn round and glance at her daughter.

. . . sixteen, seventeen, eighteen . . . Brinda had been mentally counting the nagalinga flowers over and over from the beginning. Now, counting for the umpteenth time, her mind stopped at eighteen.

"Oh please, what sort of talk is that? If we hadn't been keen about this alliance would we have proceeded in the matter at all? Please don't misunderstand what I said . . ." The girl's father smiled anxiously. "If you don't wish to help our son, let's say no more about it. Let us not break off the marriage negotiations for that reason."

. . . eighteen, nineteen, twenty, twenty-one, twenty-two. No, not that one. That was just a bud. The next now. Twenty-two, twenty-three, twenty-four, twenty-five . . .

"Good. *Now* you are talking sense. After all, why should we educate your son?"

"I have already said we'll drop the matter."

"Then everything is settled."

"Yes, settled. Only . . ."

"What now?"

"I have made no secret of my circumstances. So . . . it would be a great help if you would come forward in your generosity to cut down a bit . . . say, some five thousand rupees . . . from the agreed sum . . ."

"You have a nerve, I must say! Are you crazy? Even ten thousand is a pittance. Don't forget we are the boy's party. We could demand so much more from a girl's people just to cover what our son's education cost us . . ."

"True enough. Still, five thousand isn't much to forgo in view of the girl's good looks."

"I've seen better looks."

"Didn't you admit that she was good-looking?"

"Not bad-looking. But certainly no beauty. Her skin is brown."

"Is complexion everything? The Mahabharata describes Draupadi as incomparably beautiful. And what was her complexion? Dark, if you please! Dark! Skin color isn't important. Look at our Brinda's features—every one of them perfect, as if chiseled! Couldn't you cut down at least four thousand . . ."

"Do you know how absolutely beautiful these nagalinga flowers are?" Brinda's voice cut into the exchange. "People walk down the street gazing at this house. And every one in ten is sure to come in to ask for a few of them to be used in worship. I believe these flowers are especially suited for the worship of Shiva—no wonder! This itself is a lingam, isn't it, and may even be worshipped as such. My mother worships God daily, did you know that? Isn't that so, Amma? Not only Shiva, she worships all the gods with these flowers. And it makes the whole room smell so sweet, so sweet. Perhaps the fragrance from the tree reached you as you entered the gate? But the next day, when they wilt, they have a strong, unpleasant odor. And the petals will come loose and drop off, just like that, if you so much as touch them. But when they are fresh, what lovely, lovely flowers they are! Worthy to be offered in worship. To be sought after by people passing by who come in and ask for them for Shiva. After all, there are many other flowers that can be offered to the gods—jasmines, roses, champacs—but no! This nagalinga is superior to them all."

The girl's mother never raised her eyes.

"Look at her eyes and her hair!" exclaimed the girl's father. "You'll never have your fill! A girl so lovely, so good and competent and intelligent—one might accept such a bride without demanding any money at all but I do not ask for that, do I? I am only requesting you to reduce the total amount by just four thousand . . . or even three . . ." The girl's father glanced at the boy's leg. The boy was not paying any attention to what was going on. His eyes were glued to the girl.

And the girl's eyes were glued to the nagalinga tree. Clusters of buds, green like raw fruit, were visible on the tips of branches. Blossoms in embryo. Future flowers.

The boy's mother spoke sharply, "All said and done, he is a man. What does a man's appearance matter? Is he not educated? Is he not employed? And yet we took everything into consideration and settled for a mere ten thousand rupees instead of demanding thirty or forty thousand. How can you haggle over *that*?"

The girl's father turned to his daughter, "Brinda, my dear, why are you in this heavy Chinnalampat sari? Go, change into the georgette that your friend Minakshi gave you last week. Don't you want to show it to Aunty? Get up."

Brinda did not stir.

"Get up and go in now, will you?"

Brinda shut her eyes for a moment, tight, then opened them again. She got up and went into an inner room.

"There is a Chettiar girl named Minakshi who is a close friend of our Brinda's. Very close indeed, the two of them, since their childhood. Whenever Minakshi goes to Singapore or some other place, she never fails to bring back a present for her dear friend. Any number of georgette and nylex saris. Her father is an affluent man . . ."

Brinda came back, clad in the georgette sari. The thin material clung to her body and clearly underlined her physical charms. The boy's eyes widened. The girl's father watched him from the corner of his eye and addressed his parents. "Don't you think it is a pretty sari? Minakshi just dotes on Brinda. Presses gifts on her. Won't take no for an answer. A good girl, that."

Brinda was about to sit down.

"Just a minute, Brinda," called her father. "I left a little packet of Sovereign betel powder on the table over there. Would you mind bringing it to me?"

Brinda walked up to the table at the other end of the room and walked back. The boy's eyes followed her all the way.

"There isn't any betel powder there."

"Oh dear, I must have already finished it. How forgetful of me! That's all right, sit down now."

Brinda sat down and the boy's eyes sat down with her.

The girl's mother got up abruptly and left the room.

"Yes, my daughter has a rich friend but I am a poor man all the same," said the girl's father. "I have proceeded in this matter purely out of the desire to see my daughter married. My family is large. My wife is sick. Ten thousand rupees is a sum quite beyond my means. I'll have to borrow the money. How am I going to repay it? The very thought makes me shudder . . . Couldn't raise the amount even by selling myself . . . I appeal to your kindness. I promise to perform the marriage with all religious rites and not scrimp on the essentials. A concession of just three thousand rupees would be a great help . . ."

"Out of the paltry ten thousand agreed on? If that is the way you feel, let us call off the whole . . ."

Even before the boy's mother finished speaking, the boy spoke up, "So what's wrong with cutting down on the amount, Amma? It is all right, sir. We'll accept seven thousand."

His parents, aghast, swung around and glowered at him. Brinda began to study the nagalinga tree again.

"What are you blabbing, you fellow?"

"I am not, Amma. The poor gentleman is pleading so hard. Can we remain unmoved?"

"A lordly benefactor, aren't you?" his father snapped at him. "You fool . . ."

The boy held up his hand. "It is *my* marriage, after all. If I have no objection to this, why should you bother?"

The boy's father was dumbfounded.

Brinda counted the nagalinga flowers feverishly. One, two, three, four . . .

The manner in which the three thousand rupees were to be slashed from the budget was decided between the parties by mutual agreement. The boy's party then took their leave, asking the girl's father to have an auspicious date set for the wedding.

The girl's mother had come out again at the last minute for the formality of seeing the visitors off. When they left, she raised her head and looked straight into her husband's eyes.

He turned away. "Don't look at me like that. I know my place is reserved in the blackest hell. I'm going to the park for a stroll." He thrust his feet into his slippers and rushed out of the house and down the street, as if fleeing from himself.

The girl's mother turned toward her daughter. Then she looked away, teetered, and sat down.

"There are quite a lot of flowers on the nagalinga tree today, Amma. Plenty of them high up and many strewn on the ground too. I am going to count the whole lot. There must be at least four dozen flowers in all, if not six." Brinda looked hard at the tree. She must count the flowers. Must count the flowers. That was all. Count the flowers. She must observe the flowers with care and count them correctly . . .

. . . nine, ten, eleven, twelve, thirteen, fourteen . . . There were sure to be four dozen flowers, no doubt about that . . . twenty-five, twenty-six, twenty-seven, twenty-eight . . . And even as she was counting, suddenly the flowers seemed to vanish and she saw on the tree four dozen lame legs.

Translated from the original Tamil by the author

Indira Goswami

The Offspring

Pitambar Mahajan was sitting in front of his house. His shoes were covered with a thick layer of mud, but he did not remove them. He looked at them with pride—only he and the Gossain of the Satra possessed shoes in this remote village.

Pitambar was in his early fifties. Once a robust man, his worries had slowly emaciated his healthy body. Folds of skin hung loose beneath his chin. He talked to others with eyes averted and head bowed. His gaze was always directed to the ground beneath his feet as if he were looking for something.

Heavy rain had soaked the ground and water had collected on both sides of the village. Half-naked children played in the water or stood here and there, fishing with bamboo poles in their hands. With the rains, there was a rank growth everywhere of all sorts of plants and creepers like halechi and nalakochu. Flying frogs leaped from puddle to puddle and sometimes hit against the legs of passers-by.

Pitambar was staring intently at a chubby, naked boy trying to disentangle his fishing line from the leaves of a nalakochu plant. Suddenly his thoughts were interrupted by the grating voice of the village priest, Krishnakanta. "You have no child to call your own! Why do you devour that child with envious eyes? Each time I have gone to and returned from the temple, I have seen you sitting there like this! What about your wife? Is she better now?"

Pitambar replied hesitantly, "Several times I have taken her to the Civil Hospital at Gauhati, but it is useless. Her whole body is swelling up now."

"So there is no hope of an issue, is there? Very sad, indeed. There will be no one to continue your family line."

Pitambar remained silent. The priest stood near him for some time. He was wearing an old dhoti well above his knees, and a punjabi made of endi cloth the color of dried sheepskin. His shoulders were covered with a cotton chaddar. As Krishnakanta had only two teeth left in his mouth, his cheeks had caved in and created two hollows in his face. When he spoke, his face presented a peculiarly comic expression. His small eyes always shone with a cunning glint. His sparse hair was parted in the middle. He bent down and whispered in Pitambar's ears, "What about another marriage, eh?"

Pitambar removed his chaddar and wiped his face with one end. Before he could reply, the eyes of the two men were drawn toward a young woman passing by. She was Damayanti, the widow of a young priest from the Satra. Her rain-drenched clothes clung to her body. The color of her skin was like the dazzling foam of boiling sugarcane juice. Though her figure was rather ample, she was immensely attractive. People said all sorts of things about her. Some even called her a prostitute. Perhaps the first Brahman prostitute of the Satra!

Krishnakanta called out, "Hey, Damayanti, where are you coming from?"

"Can't you see these cocoons?"

"So, now you have started mixing with that crowd of Marwari merchants, eh! When the need arises, one stoops to washing even goats' legs as the saying goes, is it not?"

Damayanti did not reply, but bent down to squeeze out the water from the wet folds of her mekhala. Her blouse had stretched tight and was pulled up, revealing the white flesh which, to the two men, looked as tempting as the meat dressed and hung up on iron hooks in a butcher's shop! Krishnakanta turned his eyes away almost immediately, a little self-consciously, but Pitambar kept looking, enthralled by the sight. Damayanti straightened up and, without glancing at them, walked away, her mekhala rustling.

"I hear that she eats meat, fish, everything."

Krishnakanta nodded and said, "This girl has brought disgrace to Bangara Brahmans. She has thrown to the winds all restrictions and rituals prescribed for widows."

"Yes, yes! I have myself seen her once exchanging two baskets of paddy for a pair of khariya fish!"

The priest exclaimed, "Hai! hai! A widow and khariya fish! Chee, chee! Kalyuga! Kalyuga!"

"Shut up, you Brahman! Why do you want the whole world to know about a Brahman widow eating fish? It is the same everywhere, I hear. On both the north and south banks of the Brahmaputra. These old customs should be scrapped . . ."

Pitambar stopped to swat some flies buzzing around him with the corner of his chaddar. In the meantime Krishnakanta sat down with a sigh on the stump of a severed tree nearby.

Pitambar asked, "What about your jajamans for whom you perform religious ceremonies? How do they look upon you nowadays?"

"You know everything, still you ask me! My elder brother quarreled with me and made off with most of the business. I am now ruined!"

"Bapu! You don't know Sanskrit well. Your brother has spread this news everywhere and that's why your jajamans do not want you anymore."

Krishnakanta hotly denied this, "Ah! Ah! Now you tell me, how many Brahmans on the north bank can speak Sanskrit like Narahari Bhagawati? We studied together in the Sanskrit tol. He used to receive a cane beating very often but not once did I. I know why I have lost so many jajamans. Even the Brahmans well versed in all the four Vedas are starving to death. It was once easy to get a sacred thread, two dhotis, and five rupees every month from each jajaman's house. Nowadays, they don't want to observe the rituals. To avoid expenditure, our old jajaman, Manikanta Sarma, took his two sons to Kamakhya and performed their thread ceremony there! Mysanpur's jajamans have now started performing the sraddha of their fathers and mothers at the same time."

As Krishnakanta went on, Pitambar did not say one word either of assent or dissent. All the while, his mind hovered about the brief glimpse he had had of Damayanti's white flesh. He had never seen such soft, burnished flesh before. It was not as if he had not seen or touched a woman's flesh. There was his first wife, then he had brought a second one with the hope of getting a child. Now she lay bedridden with rheumatism. Her whole body had become rickety—she was like a bundle of bones dumped in a corner of the bed. He had trodden the road to the hospital at Gauhati so many times that the soles of his shoes had worn out. He was numbed by the fear that he might have to die without an issue to continue the family line.

This gnawing fear had been further heightened by the constant nagging of the priest and others, rubbing salt into his wounds. All this had upset his mental balance.

Pitambar's ailing wife, lying in bed in the mud-walled house, could see the priest standing outside. She signaled with a movement of her eyes to a servant standing nearby that he should carry one of the mooras outside for the priest to sit on. Pitambar, absorbed in himself, neither noticed the moora nor knew when and how it came to be there.

Krishnakanta stood up and said, "People of the village are gossiping about you, that you have gone off your head. What do you think? Don't you know that there are many people in this world who are childless like you? Just try to look at it in a different way. After all, it is all maya, illusion!"

Pitambar's head drooped. The priest could see the gray hair on it. His clothes looked worn and untended. Only his shoes, though muddy, were intact. He felt a kind of pity for this man. Once upon a time he was so handsome that people called him "gora paltan." Now he had money, a granary full of paddy, everything. Still he was not happy! Suddenly Krishnakanta was struck by a thought. He looked around. He could see the open door of Pitambar's bedroom and the reclining body of his wife. He could even see her eyes, burning like those of an animal in a dark jungle, as if she were straining with all her might to catch what he was saying to her husband. The intensity of those glowing eyes, even after traversing that long distance, was heartrending! The priest would not have believed it possible.

He made up his mind. Bending down, he whispered into Pitambar's ear, "I can help you out of this agony."

"Another solution?"

"Yes, this time it is absolutely pakka!"

"I don't understand you . . ."

"This time there is no question of an unsuccessful pregnancy! She has gone through four abortions and every time she has buried those evil things in the bamboo grove behind her house."

Startled, Pitambar cried out, "Are you talking about Damayanti?"

"Yes, yes! Nowadays Brahman girls are even marrying fishermen. The daughter of the Gossain on the Dhaneshwari riverbank married a Muslim boy! Gandhi Maharaj has shown us the path. That's why I am telling you . . ."

Pitambar exclaimed in a surge of excitement, "What is it you are saying?"

"If you want, you can make Damayanti your own!"

Krishnakanta turned his head and looked again toward Pitambar's bedridden wife. He could still see the two glowing embers in her face. She was staring steadfastly at him.

Pitambar stood up. Here was Krishnakanta putting what he could only dream about into clear-cut words! He went up to him, trying to seize his hand in an excess of gratitude, but Krishnakanta shrank back. He had just taken his bath and he had to go and do the daily washing-ceremony of Murlidhar in Gossain's house. If this man touched him, then he would have to bathe again.

Pitambar's condition was like that of a drowning man suddenly sighting a colorful sail. He did not know whether to touch the priest's hands or his feet.

"So you had this in mind for quite a long time, did you?"

Krishnakanta again cast a glance at the invalid woman. This time her eyes were shut tight, probably in a spasm of pain. Pitambar knelt down near the priest's feet and entreated him earnestly, "Only you can do it! Please help me with this girl! She is a Brahman. I will keep her in all comfort!"

A cunning smile played for a moment on Krishnakanta's toothless mouth. "Hm, well . . . er, I'll see about it. I'll have to come again a couple of times. Then there are her two little daughters to be taken care of."

Pitambar got up with confused emotions and made his way to the bedroom. When he entered, he saw his wife open her eyes and look at him. She now saw him opening the wooden box where they kept money and other valuables. A little later, he closed the box and went back to the priest.

Krishnakanta took the money, twenty rupees in cash, and went away humming under his breath.

A week had passed. Pitambar waited anxiously for the priest, his whole being on tenterhooks. In these past seven days, he had seen Damayanti passing by his house on her way to Gossain's place, carrying cotton for making sacred threads. The sight of her body heightened the turmoil in his mind. His obsession for her created strange hallucinations. Before his maddened eyes, Damayanti's clothes seemed to disappear each time revealing more and more of her beautiful white-fleshed body.

People said that she was born at Rauta on the banks of the Dhaneshwari river in Kamrup. There is a belief that nowhere else can you find girls as beautiful as the Brahman girls born on the banks of the Dhaneshwari. Pitambar was now convinced that this was absolutely true.

Pitambar started sitting outside his house every day. At this time of the year, Damayanti came regularly to gather kollmu and other vegetables that grew wild along the drains bordering the road. Her two little daughters, skinny and naked, usually trailed behind her. Their thin and undernourished bodies looked incongruous against their mother's healthy and voluptuous body. Damayanti's long and reddish-brown hair often caught Pitambar's eyes.

One day Pitambar gathered enough courage to go near her when she was plucking green leaves and said, "You will catch cold if you stand like this in muddy water every day."

Damayanti looked back, her eyes opening wide with astonishment. But she did not reply.

Pitambar said again, "I'll send the servant. You tell him to collect as many greens as you want and . . ."

But his sentence remained unfinished. She looked back and Pitambar's eyes fell before her intense, disdainful gaze. He left the place hurriedly and went and sat down on the tree stump in front of his house. He could see his wife lying again on the bed like a bird with broken wings. In the morning she had seemed better, even moved around the room a little, but now the bed had claimed her again. Anger welled up inside him. He threw a look of undiluted fury in her direction. Sometimes he felt he could hear her dried-up joints creaking in her ailing frame. He looked at her with disgust. It was time for the next dose of her medicine but he did not get up. He looked at his shoes, took out his handkerchief, and started cleaning them. He glanced often at the road, impatient for the sight of Krishnakanta. Suddenly he heard the *krr krr* sound of cart wheels. He knew what it was. His tenants were bringing his share of Boka Bhan, that variety of rice harvested in July, grown on his land. Normally, he would have been very happy at the sight of the carts laden with paddy. He would inhale with great pleasure and satisfaction the fresh fragrance of newly harvested paddy and rush to the carts to count the number of baskets as they were unloaded. But today he remained where he was. His servants, however, came out immediately and started carrying the baskets to the granary. When this was done, the tenants were offered tea, jaggery, and parched rice, which they gulped down with obvious enjoyment. They then went to the well, washed their hands, and partook of the pan and betel nuts kept separately for them. The tenants now approached Pitambar to take leave of him, but were perturbed to find him indifferent and unresponsive. "Ah! You don't have children. All your granaries are now overflowing with paddy! Who will eat it? And you are growing old. Now is the time to worship god and offer charity and alms," they seemed to be saying.

Pitambar went inside the house and brought out the money. He made their payment one by one and sent them off in complete silence. He then returned to his original place and sat down again. His eyes turned to the open door through which he could see his bedridden wife. Her eyes were open. A tumbler lay below the bed. Perhaps she had taken a drink of water. It was long past her usual medicine time.

Pitambar got up to go inside and give her the medicine. He removed his shoes and placed them in a corner. As he was about to cross the threshold, he heard a coughing behind him. Krishnakanta at last! He ran back and put on his shoes. His wife's eyes had followed him, expecting her medicine, but now she closed them again wearily. The fire in her eyes was extinguished, only the ashes remained.

Pitambar asked impatiently, "Bapu! What news have you brought for me? Tell me quickly!"

In his excitement he even forgot to offer him a seat.

"Tell me! What is the news?"

The priest glanced round in all four directions. The invalid was lying on her bed like a corpse. She was not going to hear anything!

He whispered into Pitambar's ears, "Just listen! I have dug up some information. Right now her womb is empty—it is not even one month since she buried the evil fruit of her last adventure. Her little daughter said that this time her mother had used a crowbar given by that student who goes to Sariali college on bicycle, to dig the grave. He is a boy without character from a very rich household. During college hours, he used to go straight to Damayanti's place and hide his textbooks in the basket of rice. His college fees went for her cosmetics."

The priest lowered his voice still further and barely whispered, "On the bare floor! In front of the little girls! Hari, Hari! They copulated shamelessly. This time it was obviously that student's child."

Pitambar heard everything in ice-cold silence.

The priest continued, "I told her about you. She was infuriated! She spat out. 'That pariah! How dare he send this proposal to me! Doesn't he know that I am from the jajamani Brahman caste and he, the vermin, is a low-caste Mahajan?' I told her that when she was wallowing in the slime of sin, how could she talk of high caste or low caste? She was not getting any proposals for marriage from Brahman boys. Who will marry a widow? That, too, with daughters? At least you are prepared to marry her, who is like a piece of sugarcane, chewed and thrown away. I told her straightaway that you would take the Panchayat's consent, arrange a havan, and marry her with due formalities. She questioned me about your wife. I told her that your wife was like a straw which may be blown away anytime, that you would keep her in great comfort. I even told her you were the only man in the Satra who wears a pair of costly shoes! Suddenly she started crying. I don't know why she cried. Then she wiped away her tears with her chaddar and said, 'Nowadays, I don't keep well. I would like to lean on something solid and permanent.' I told her, 'How can you remain in good health? I have heard that you have got rid of those evil things from your womb four or five times. If the Panchayat takes up this matter, it will be a terrible thing for the Satra. Even if somebody goes to your door for a glass of water, he will be fined twenty rupees. You have been spared only because you are a Brahman. But for how long?' She replied, 'What can I do? I had to live. They even stopped their orders for sacred threads and puffed rice. They considered me impure, contaminated! And those tenants! They have turned thieves and don't give me my share of paddy. They take advantage of my helplessness. In these circumstances, where should I have gone with my two tiny daughters? I have not paid the land revenue. The land, too, will be auctioned off! What can I do?'"

Pitambar grew impatient. "What about my proposal?"

"Yes, yes! I am coming to that. She wants to meet you. On the full moon night. At her dhekal, the room in the backyard for pounding the paddy."

Pitambar was overwhelmed. Krishnakanta took this opportunity to whisper in his ears, "Come, take out forty rupees for me! The mosquitoes are playing havoc. I want to buy a mosquito net."

Pitambar went inside the house. He saw that his wife was awake. He did not care and went straight to the wooden box. He took out the money and turned round to go out of the room. The sick woman was staring at him. He burst out enraged, "Why are you staring at me like that? I will scoop out your eyes!"

Krishnakanta heard everything, understood everything. Taking the money, he whispered to Pitambar, "Look, if she stares too much, give her a dose of opium. Like your first wife, she is not quarrelsome. She probably feels deeply guilty for not bearing you a child."

And he laughed toothlessly. The invalid lying on her bed closed her eyes again. The priest, becoming serious, continued, "But that bitch, Damayanti, has great hunger for money! It's all right now. You can touch her in the dhekal . . ."

Pitambar threw a glance at the sleeping woman inside. Even from that distance he could clearly see small beads of perspiration on her forehead.

It was a full moon night in the month of August. Pitambar took out his best clothes. He lovingly wiped his shoes clean with his hand. He took the looking glass out into the open yard and scanned his face. He had shaved in the morning. Peering into the glass, he saw the crisscross of wrinkles on his face. He thought it looked like a fish caught in a net.

He set out for Damayanti's house. He had to cross a thick sal forest. Her house lay beyond the forest on the outer edge of the village. It was an ideal place for Damayanti to carry out her nefarious activities.

In the moonlit sky, he could see mushroom-colored clouds shaped like a canon. He felt that the moon looked like somebody had skinned and quartered a deer and placed it in the sky. It was so temptingly lustrous. Suddenly the moon became the naked voluptuous body of Damayanti in Pitambar's eyes. He tried to imagine the shape of her breasts. They would be like the soft, rounded stomach of a pregnant goat. And the shaft of her body like a tender bamboo shoot. He lowered his eyes. No, no, he could not look at the sky any longer. He walked faster. Near the sal forest, a pack of jackals flashed across the path. He reached the gate. Silently he slipped inside and entered the courtyard. He saw the dim kerosene lamp burning in one room. He peered in and saw a child fast asleep near a cluster of jackfruit and baskets of rice. The other girl was writing something on a small slate.

Damayanti was observing his movements from the dhekal. She called out, "Hey! Here! This way!"

Like a duty-bound soldier, he turned round on the quick and went toward her. A clay lamp of mustard-oil was burning near the pounding horse. She was leaning against a ramshackle wall. Pitambar did not dare look into her eyes: he was afraid. Suddenly it struck him that it was all an illusion! Her figure before him in the dim light was also an illusion. But his thoughts were cut short. He heard her say, "Have you brought some money?"

He was stunned. He did not expect her first question to be this. He said quickly, "Here! Take this! Whatever I have is yours now." He took out a small string purse from his waist and put it in her hand. Damayanti thrust the purse into the cleavage of her blouse. She took the lamp and guided him to the room where earlier the little girl had been doing her lessons. They found both girls fast asleep, clinging to each other. Damayanti then took Pitambar to an adjacent room, damp and dark. In it was a low cot, made of guava wood. It had been given to her deceased husband at the time of Gossain's funeral ceremony. She blew out the lamp . . .

Two months had passed. It was late evening. Pitambar left the dark in haste to get back to his house. Damayanti went to the well languidly and started taking a bath. Just then, the priest entered the courtyard. He remarked sarcastically, "You never used to take a bath after sleeping with the Brahman boy. What has happened now?"

Damayanti did not reply.

"Eh! He is from the lower caste, is that it . . . ?"

Suddenly Damayanti came running out as she was, in drenched clothes, and rushed to the far corner of the courtyard. She bent over and started vomiting. Krishnakanta stood still for a moment, stupefied. Then he shuffled up to her and said gently, "This must surely be Pitambar's . . ."

Damayanti still remained silent. "Ah! This is good news indeed! That man was yearning for a child."

Even now she did not say a word.

"So I will go now and give him the good news. He can now wed you openly."

He came up to her and whispered, "People are shocked and horrified by what is going on in this house. There was talk, off and on, of calling a meeting of the Panchayat. And listen! There was another thing. Something very serious! That three-month-old fetus you buried behind the bijulee bamboos . . . one day a fox dug it out, swallowed part of it and left a half-eaten limb in the Gossain's priest's courtyard. You know, the one who washes the Gossain's Murlidhar. He had a hard time getting himself purified—had to swallow two glasses of cow dung water."

Damayanti started vomiting again, making sounds of *auk auk*, her mouth wide open.

The priest continued, "Knowing all this, Pitambar is prepared to marry you. Listen, with my hands on the sacred thread, I tell you, this time if you do not save yourself from sin by taking this chance, you will surely burn in hellfire!"

After giving the best news of his life to Pitambar, Krishnakanta said, "So, at last, your dreams may come true. If she does not destroy this child, then you can rest assured that she will marry you."

Pitambar was sitting on the tree stump in front of his house, as usual, wearing his prized possession—his shoes. When he heard Krishnakanta's words, his whole body trembled. Was it really true? Could it be his own, his very own child in that woman's womb? It must be the truth! This Brahman could not possibly utter lies. It is really my child!

He stood up, restless and agitated, and started pacing up and down in front of his house.

Krishnakanta said, "At this age! To become a father! It's really a fortune, a miracle!"

Pitambar kneeled at the priest's feet and entreated, "Please, Bapu! Don't let my hopes be shattered. You know my background. My forefathers were brave warriors. They fought those Burmese invaders. You know that! If this lineage is snapped, if there is no son to carry it forward, only this doomed sufferer knows what tortures my soul will go through. And now this seductive sorceress holds my life in her fist. Oh Bapu, tell me! What should I do?"

Krishnakanta lifted one hand in consolation and said, "Like the vulture keeping vigil over a corpse, I'll guard that woman. Not only that, I'll issue a strict warning to that old hag not to give her any of her evil herbs and roots for an abortion. But all this is not possible without money. I'll require lots of money!"

This time, Pitambar did not have to go inside the house for it. Only that morning, he had sold all the jackfruit from his seven trees to a merchant from Orput, and he had the entire roll of currency notes in his pocket. He took it out and placed it in Krishnakanta's outstretched palm. The priest blessed him and left.

When Pitambar entered his house he again encountered the piercing, unblinking gaze of the sick woman. He was perturbed by those accusing eyes but only for a moment. Then he was his usual blunt and callous self again. He growled, "You barren bitch! Why are you staring at me like that?"

Pitambar became almost insane with happiness. He would sit in his favorite place outside the house and dream about his child in Damayanti's womb. He imagined the different stages of his growth: he dreamed that his son, in the flush of youth, was taking him for a walk along the river bank. It appeared to him that the long golden thread of his family lineage was pulling them forward into a glorious future. He dreamed that both father and son were moving into a bright light where heaven and earth fused together on the distant horizon.

With the help of his servant he took out an old box perched on the rafter of his bedroom. He cleaned the dust and the cobwebs sticking to the box and, taking it to a corner of the room, opened it stealthily. Inside there was a package wrapped in cloth. It contained some half-burned pieces of his father's bones and a string of gold beads his father used to wear around his neck. On his deathbed, his father had given the string to him, telling him that the gold beads would be like golden steps which his son would mount, carrying the family flag.

Pitambar gazed at the relics for some time, then repacked them carefully in the same cloth and placed the box in its original place on the rafter.

Days passed. Pitambar became impatient. He had heard that a five-month-old fetus in a mother's womb cannot be destroyed. He waited, nervous and agitated, for this precarious period to be over. Each day was like a mountain that stood before him. Every day he imagined that he heard the footsteps of the girl coming toward him. He heard her telling him to make arrangements for the havan. She would say plaintively, "I cannot stir out of the house now. Look how big my stomach has grown. I have been thinking! Hindu, Muslim, Brahman, or Kayastha. All these are like pieces of an earthen pot. There is no meaning in these words. I only want a man from whose body real blood flows when his flesh is cut open."

In Pitambar's overwrought mind, the specter of Damayanti became all too vivid and beautiful. He even imagined that he heard the musical notes of anklets from her smooth bamboo shoot–like ankles.

Three months passed. Now almost every day Pitambar strolled along the banks of the Dhaneshwari with the youthful son of his hallucinations. The dream pursued him persistently, day and night.

It was the month of August. The storm had broken in the afternoon and it was raining heavily. Pitambar went to the room near the dhekal to close the door. His wife was staring at him. He stood still. The wide open eyes were like shining snakes in the dark. Suddenly, the storm lashed out. All the oil lamps flickered and died out. It was pitch-black. Over the roar of the storm, he heard crashing sounds. What was that? Surely lightning had struck a tree in his courtyard and split it in two. Which tree was it? he wondered. He rushed out helter-skelter. His servants were already there shifting the heap of coconuts from the veranda to the dhekal.

Gradually the thunder and lightning abated, but the rain continued to come down in sheets. Suddenly Pitambar heard somebody calling out to him. Lantern in hand, he rushed out to see who it was. A figure loomed into view, completely drenched, dhoti held high above his knees. He had an old torn umbrella in his hand. The man was very thin, almost skeletal. He came toward Pitambar. What was it now? Holding the lantern higher, Pitambar looked closely at him. It was Krishnakanta! Pitambar exclaimed. "Bapu, you? What is it? Why have you come in this foul weather?"

With great difficulty the priest reached the veranda and shut his umbrella. His hands were trembling. He looked extremely agitated. He squeezed out the water from his dhoti and said, "Your first wife died under an inauspicious star, Pitambar. That must be the reason for what has happened now."

"What? What did you say? What is wrong now?"

"It is said in the Shastras that when a person dies under this star even the shortest blade of grass in the courtyard burns to ashes. For you now, everything has become ashes!"

Pitambar cried out in alarm, "What has happened? For God's sake, tell me quickly!"

"Alas! She has destroyed it. She has got rid of the unborn child. She will not carry the seed of a low caste. She is a Brahman of Shandilya gotra. Oh, Pitambar! Pitambar! She has destroyed your child!"

The youth walking along the Dhaneshwari had suddenly slipped and fallen into the river . . .

One day, in the middle of the night, Damayanti woke up with a start, disturbed by some sounds coming from the backyard, as if someone was digging up the earth. Alarmed and frightened, she woke up her elder daughter. Both strained their ears. Yes, yes, there were distinct sounds of digging coming from the direction of the bamboo grove behind the house. That was the very spot where both mother and daughter had, some nights before, dug a pit for the aborted child! Yes, that was the night when both mother and daughter were terrified by the frequent howling of the foxes as the daughter held the earthen lamp and Damayanti dug the earth with a crowbar in jerking movements and scooped out the loose earth with nervous hands.

Thuk! Thuk! Thuk!

They opened the window cautiously and looked out. They saw a man digging in the dim light of a lantern hung from a bamboo tree nearby.

Damayanti's heart started beating fast. Was it Pitambar out there? Yes, it was! He was digging the earth with single-minded determination. Gradually, the tempo of the digging increased. The Mahajan's whole body and face assumed a terrible, violent aspect. He dug and clawed the earth frantically with frenzied energy.

Damayanti's body started trembling from head to foot. Her heart beat violently. What should she do? Should she shout? Should she keep quiet? A terrible thing was happening!

"Mahajan! Mahajan!"

There was no response!

Thuk! Thuk! Thuk! Thuk!

"Why are you digging, Mahajan?"

Pitambar looked up, but did not reply.

Thuk! Thuk! Thuk! Thuk!

Damayanti became frantic. She shouted furiously, "What will you get from there? Yes, I have buried it! It was a boy! But he is just a lump of flesh, blood, and mud! Stop it! Stop it!"

Pitambar raised his head. His eyes were burning. "I'll touch that flesh with these hands of mine. He was the scion of my lineage, a part of my flesh and blood! I will touch him!"

Translated from the original Assamese by the author

Dhiruben Patel

Crushed Flowers

"Kushi, don't go near him just now. You'll only upset him," said her mother, and snatched the medicine bottle from her hand.

In a way she was right. There was no reason to feel hurt, yet Kushi felt a tingling sensation in her eyes. A few seconds more and the tears would come gushing out.

She ran out of the room, into the narrow corridor which had a sackful of coal and a tin of kerosene in one corner. Never mind, one corner is free. One could sit there and look at the neighbor's garden. It was a beautiful garden, always green, luxuriating in its solitary happiness. The gardener, too, always looked happy . . . could it be because of the garden? Wiping her eyes with the back of her hand, she thought she must ask him the next time she got a chance. But what was the use of asking? Would anyone let her become a gardener? It's disastrous to be a girl. One can't be a gardener, or a tonga-walla, or even a cobbler sitting on the footpath repairing people's shoes. One can't even dream of so many interesting careers. Kushi stared at the garden with a crestfallen face. By this time the gardener had come quite close. He was cutting flowers from the rosebush. He looked at Kaushambi, gave her a smile, and extended his hand. She too leaned out and, as usual, stretched out her hand to him. That was when Vishu crept up on her.

"Kushi! Hasn't Mother asked you not to indulge in such antics?"

"Oh, yes . . ."

"Then how come . . .?

Vaishali was only fifteen months younger than Kaushambi, but because she was younger she was supposed to be more innocent and thus authorized to scold Kaushambi as freely as their mother did. Kaushambi reluctantly left the corridor and entered the room.

"Kushi!"

"Yes?"

"The doctor must have given you the medicine immediately?"

"Eh? Oh, yes, he did."

"And he couldn't have asked for money?"

"No, but I promised to pay him next week."

"From where are we going to get the money?"

"I don't know, but if we do get it from somewhere, we can pay him."

"Somewhere? What does that mean?" asked Vaishali.

She would go on questioning Kushi until she got a proper answer, and then dutifully report the conversation to their mother. She was right, though, there was no possibility of getting any money next week, unless . . .

"Raman Uncle might come," Kaushambi blurted out.

"He's not going to come soon, and even if he does he won't give us any money this time."

"Why? He did last time."

"Why should anybody give us money all the time? Kushi, tell me, why does the doctor always give you medicine without taking any money?"

"Because he is a good man. He's kindhearted and he loves people."

"Then why doesn't he give *me* free medicine?"

She knew why. The doctor liked Kushi. Whenever she went to him he smiled and talked to her and never mentioned all the unpaid bills. He never asked, but she always said, "I will pay next week." "All right," he would say, and continue examining the other patients. She couldn't understand why her mother and Vishu didn't like him. But then, they didn't like many people: the neighbor's gardener; the postman; the milkman; Durga Prasad, the owner of the mobile library; Ravi, who stayed on the first floor; Tara Aunty's son, Viral; or the vegetable vendor from Bassein. But Kaushambi liked them all and all of them liked her. Mother always told her not to smile at them or talk to them—it was not proper. But Kaushambi couldn't help herself, and this always upset her mother, and Vishu took her cue from her. Kaushambi became very quiet and thoughtful. She decided that if her mother didn't like it, she should give up smiling at everybody, even Vishu and Mother herself. At such moments, tears would well up in her eyes, but as soon as someone turned up and hailed her, "Hi, Kushi! How are you?" she couldn't help smiling back and responding, "I'm fine!"

It was beyond her to pull a long face or stop talking to people. She showered smiles like the parijat tree that showers flowers for no reason. It is impossible to pick them up and paste them back onto the tree. The flowers would be trod upon or muddied—others will still fall, equally beautiful, delicate, totally pure . . .

Mother couldn't forget that Kaushambi is a girl, seventeen years old, completely unselfconscious, smiling, and talking to anybody who comes along. Whenever she was scolded she would become serious and say, "I'm sorry, I won't do it again," but as soon as the opportunity arose, she would, of course, do just that.

Vaishali, too, is a girl, but quite the opposite. Nobody would dare look at her twice. She suspects the whole world. Although she did her level best to curb Kaushambi, she was, after all, the younger sister and couldn't be as firm as she would have liked.

If only they had some money, Mother would have gotten her married off somehow or the other. But there is none. There is a home to maintain, two young girls, sixteen and seventeen, and a father. There are some bottles of medicine for TB and there is a sickbed. Nobody knows when the sickbed will no longer be necessary. Until then this home requires milk and fruit and butter and nutritious food. This is the demand made by an incessant cough, a shameless and continuous demand. Everyone has to bow down to its raucous command. No marriage can be arranged until its demands cease. Either for Kushi or for Vishu. The realization of this burns like a furnace in the mother's heart, which is why her words are like burning cinders.

But Kushi does not know all this—she just keeps getting burned. Still, Mother's words don't scorch as much as Vishu's questions.

"Why did Viral smile at you?"

"Who gave you this rose?"

"Did anyone come here this afternoon?"

"Look, Kushi, isn't that Ravi staring at our house?"

"Why did the vegetable vendor take only fifteen paise from you?"

"Why did you wear a sari today?"

Kushi has no answers. Her replies become the springboard for more questions. At such moments, the petals of her smile crumple, and she moves from place to place in this cramped house, trying to find a lonely corner for herself. Sometimes she feels like going near the sickbed and sitting there. She remembers that she loved her father very much when she was a young girl. He was tall and handsome and his clothes and hands exuded a typical fragrance. It was a mixture of tobacco, eau de cologne, and pan. She loved to dive deep into his happy laughter, flowing like a rippling stream, to be lifted up in his strong arms and try hard to answer his strange questions. At that time she had been a child and her father had liked her. Now that she had grown up, he didn't talk much with her anymore. He rarely looked at her and when he did, it was the look of a stranger, anxious and apprehensive. That cough and emaciated body belonged to her father. That voice full of complaints also belonged to her father, as did the ugly face . . . but Kushi only remembered her childhood and the laughter that lighted it up like the sun.

Perhaps her own unstoppable smiles were a tiny rivulet of that river.

Just as that had dried up, this too might succumb to old age, sickness, or poverty. The thought of it frightened her considerably.

Why did Mother and Vishu not think of this possibility? They can see quite clearly that the ocean does not even murmur any longer. This can happen to anybody, anytime. Don't they know? Kushi is afraid of this; that is why she wants to laugh while she can. She doesn't mind whether it is the postman, the gardener, or the milkman standing before her. She doesn't care about the faces. She just looks at the eyes, full of warmth, full of life. She cannot help responding to the sunrise in their eyes. Let Mother worry about her. Let Vishu prepare a bed of arrows with her piercing questions. She can lie down on it, but as long as her roots are alive, she will not perish, will not turn to stone. No doubt stones are very useful things, so much better than trees. Houses can be built with them, immovable and permanent. Flowers would not fall around them, there would be no dirt. But stones can crumble. Why does Mother not think of that?

"Kushi!"

"Yes?"

"Go and get the evening paper from Mena masi."

"Shall I get it from Tara masi instead?"

"Why? That good-for-nothing fellow might be at home."

Mother's objection was beyond her comprehension. Why shouldn't a person be in his own home? Was it an offense? It seemed to be a crime in Mother's opinion. A sort of devilry. It was imperative that Viral not be at home when Kushi went to borrow the newspaper.

Mena masi stayed on the ground floor. Kaushambi was on her way there when Viral hailed her from the first floor.

"Hi, Kushi! Where are you going?"

"To Mena masi's, to borrow the newspaper."

"Here it is, take it."

It was true that Viral was always overjoyed to see Kaushambi. Now Kushi couldn't understand why anybody should object to someone being happy. This was a riddle that was just beyond her. She took the newspaper from Viral and said, "I'll bring it back soon." She knew that as soon as she entered her own home her mother would ask her where she had got it from, and her reply would make her unhappy and angry. But how could she displease Viral?

"Kaushambi!" The landlord's son, Madhu, met her on the way. They lived on the second floor of that chal, in the last three or four rooms. Madhu was very good-looking. He looked even better now that he had stopped having his hair cut. For some time now, he hasn't called her "Kushi." She stopped and smiled, "Hello! What do you want?"

"Where did you go?"

"To borrow a newspaper."

"We get newspapers every day, and in the morning we get two. If you want, I'll bring one for you."

"Oh, okay."

"Kaushambi!"

"Yes."

"I've got a beautiful watch. I'd like you to take it."

"Why? Don't you like it?"

Madhu's face fell. Kaushambi didn't want it. Immediately she smiled and said, "No, no, it's wonderful, but you keep it."

"But you do like it?"

"Of course."

"Okay, then do me a favor. Wear it just for today. Then you can give it back. Okay?"

"But, why?"

"Oh, please wear it. Just to make me happy."

If such a small thing could make someone happy, where was the harm? Kaushambi smiled and took the watch. She could return it the next morning when she went to get the milk.

"Madhu!"

"Yes?"

"Will you come tomorrow morning to buy milk?"

Madhu didn't like getting up early but he couldn't refuse. He nodded.

"I'll return the watch then."

"All right."

Kushi saw Vaishali approaching, no doubt to inquire about the delay, so she moved away quickly. She barely heard Madhu's last words, "You're very nice."

Kaushambi's smile was wiped clean. The whole world might say so, but she knew that Mother didn't think she was a nice girl, nor her father, nor Vishu. No member of her own family liked her. How did it matter, what outsiders said? Her mother was right: how could they be trusted?

Why did these things happen only to her? Wouldn't it have been much better if Madhu had given the watch to Vishu? Of course, Vishu would never have accepted it—she was much too sensible.

"Kushi!"

"Yes?"

"Why are you so late?"

"Am I late?"

"Of course!"

Kaushambi simply handed her the paper in reply.

"Kushi!"

"Yes?"

"How is Mena masi?"

"I don't know."

"What do you mean? Where did you get the paper from?"

"From Viral's place."

"Didn't I tell you not to go there?"

Kaushambi quivered before her mother's angry gaze. She was now thoroughly convinced that she had committed a heinous crime. She looked down at the floor and said in a very small voice, "I didn't go there. He called me and gave it to me."

"That is precisely what I want to know. Why does he behave like this? Why did he call you?"

Kaushambi was silent. "Kushi! Look up. Answer me! Why does everyone only call you and not the other girls?"

Kaushambi looked up. There was fear in her mother's eyes, but it was barely visible, like a serpent coiled near the roots of a tree. That which was visible was dislike, hatred for this young girl, a strong suspicion which had no beginning or end, nor any shape either.

"Go and return the newspaper!"

Kaushambi straightened her clothes and started moving away.

"Vishu, give her the newspaper!" Mother shouted.

"I haven't read it yet."

"Never mind! Give it back."

Kaushambi took the newspaper silently, glanced at her mother, and left the room.

The wings on her feet had been clipped. It took her a very long time to reach the second floor. She would have to knock at the partition in front of Madhu's house if it was closed. Dear God, let Madhu be outside! Let the door be open! Dear God . . .

"Kaushambi!"

Thank God! "Madhu, here's your watch."

"What happened? Don't you like wearing it?"

Madhu's Taj Mahal crumbled before it had even been built. Looking at Kaushambi with a vacant gaze, he spoke as he used to earlier. "Kushi, tell me what happened?"

Kaushambi did not look at him, did not say anything. She just wept. Her throat was suffocated. She was awash in a monstrous wave of scalding hot tears which swept away her sense of time and space.

"Oh, Kushi! What has happened? Have I done anything wrong?"

If jumping from the second floor would have stopped her tears, Madhu would have certainly done so. But he didn't know what to say.

An eternity was over. All of a sudden Kaushambi stopped weeping. She thrust the wristwatch in Madhu's hands and walked away very fast, with a red face and swollen eyes. She still had to return the newspaper to Viral.

Translated from the original Gujarati by the author

Bani Basu

Aunty

The feast for the Brahmans was over yesterday. The arrangements were sumptuous. Today was the last day of mourning. No one knew how, but there were around two-hundred-and-fifty guests. Over fifty of them belonged to the clan. In addition there were the families related by marriage. And then the neighbors.

"Where would our father's prestige be, leave alone our own, if we hadn't fed them fish and rice?" said Anish.

Deepika, or Dipu, said, "Absolutely. Father was totally helpless. You men had escaped long ago. These boys of the neighborhood—Keshta, Bishtu, Gonu, Bhodor—if they hadn't been there, there probably would have been no doctor when he needed one. After all, Aunty is only a woman."

Midstream, her words hit a raw spot in Anish. Dipu was always good at being unpleasant. Hadn't he admitted already that he had done nothing? He couldn't afford to. If a man works in Hoshiarpur in Punjab, he certainly can't keep running across to Rishi Bankim Sarani in Srirampore every once in a while to look after his father. Those staying closer to home should have been the ones to come to some arrangement among themselves on this matter. The reply to Deepika's snide comment, however, came from Anish's wife, Deepika's sister-in-law. Coming from Comilla, she had a way with words. "Well, Didi," she said, "your elder brother fled a long time ago, thinking of what would be best for the family. But these days even daughters get a share of the property. Should only the sons do the looking after?"

Abashed, Deepika replied, "If only you had a charming son like mine! You would have understood then, Boudi, whatever few hours ride it is between Asansol and Srirampore, why I didn't have the opportunity to visit my father's home more often."

Atish's wife, Shukla, was the cheerful sort who didn't like quarrels and conflicts. She laughed and said, "Ever since you came, Didi, you've been concentrating your attack on Bubulram. Why? What has he done?"

"What can he possibly do? Nothing at all. Only his daily routine is written in letters of gore. Today a fishbone plants itself on his brow. Tomorrow a deuce ball hits his groin. The day after, his hand falls on the kitchen knife and out flows a river of blood. And then there is a stream of complaints—from the neighborhood, from the school. It's just that he comes first in class every year, so they don't throw him out in spite of all his devilish pranks." Dipu's face shone with pride.

"Is he that naughty? He doesn't look it though!"

Dipu was happy to have turned the course of the conversation. She hadn't really wanted to quarrel with her elder brother, although she enjoyed making a biting comment once in a while. "What do you mean, naughty?" she said. "Didn't I tell you he is an absolute devil? Keeps punching a sandbag twice a day. Then makes me squat and dashes off over my head. Says he is learning karate. And the club is an additional nuisance."

Dipu's sister Anita, or Anu, could share her elder sister's pride in her son. Usually in these matters sisters feel a sense of empathy. "Mejoboudi," she said, "did you know that Bubul was the all-Bengal champion in yoga last year? He can do such difficult asanas, you'll go crazy watching him. Worse than the circus contortionists."

Shukla opened her eyes wide, "Really, Anu! Such a young boy and so much talent! We only knew that he was good at his studies."

As the ladies had, as usual, gotten around to extolling the virtues of their offspring, Anish was about to leave the room in disgust. Atish came in to say, "Dada, what are you doing here? Father's boss, Das Sahib, and quite a few others from the office have been waiting a long time. Remember Das Sahib?"

"What are you saying, Rontu? How can I not remember him? He is the man who guided me in my youth. I sat for the competitive exam only because he said so. You should have called me."

The two brothers, looking like hermits with their shaven heads, immediately bustled out of the room, holding onto the flowing ends of their dhotis.

Out in the veranda they bumped into their youngest sister Ishita, or Itu. Up the flight of stairs was the large hall of the first floor, where the guests had gathered. Itu was looking after them. Seeing her elder brothers, she waved her arms and said, "There you are, Gaur-Nitai, alias Jagai-Madhai. Where are you off to in such a hurry? Do you realize that the first batch of guests must be fed now?"

Atish said, "You're the expert. Why don't you call Dipu, Anu, and Boudi? Don't ask Shukla, she'll end up doing everything wrong."

"Is that the truth or are you protecting your wife?" Itu made an eloquent face.

"Stop trying to be too smart. Why don't you call her and see the fun? She wouldn't know one aunt from another; she'd mix up the uncles and cousins and make such a mess that you'll be taught a lesson."

Atish didn't stop any longer. Anish had gone ahead, so he too lifted the end of his dhoti and advanced toward the stairs.

Das Sahib and the others had been there quite a while. When Anish, the eldest son of the family, got a first class with Honors in BSc, Das Sahib had driven down in his impressive car all the way from Theatre Road to Srirampore, carrying a box of cakes. He had filled the corridors of the old house with the resonance of his deep voice and said, "Rakhaharibabu, don't you send your son into the university now. Let him sit for the competitive examination."

"But with such good results! Shouldn't he study further?"

"Why? To become a clerk? Or to take a seventy-five rupee job as a schoolteacher? This is an order—Anish will sit for the administrative services examination. Forget about his MSc. Bengali boys are increasingly being left behind in the competitive examinations, Rakhaharibabu. Boys from the South, UP, and even Bihar get into the administrative services these days. And these Bengali bookworms, driven by the ghosts of Faraday and Edison, manage nothing more than their daily bread."

At the time when Anish had joined the IPS, sons of middle-class families did not think along these lines at all. Certainly not his middle-class father. Touching the feet of an octogenarian Das Sahib, Anish remembered those early days.

"Enough, enough. May you have a long life, son." Having lost his hair and teeth, the erstwhile Sahib had become a homely old Bengali gentleman. In the empty cave of his loose, hanging mouth he seemed to be perpetually chewing something. There was a walking stick in his hand. It was easy to doubt whether there was a human body at all inside the shell of the sparkling dhoti and kurta.

"Your revered father was a hundred percent honest man, honest citizen, my son. Dutiful, unselfish, concerned about the well-being of others. Who knows why he had to survive ten long years in this way after his wife's death. It's all God's will."

Anish's father-in-law was present. He said, "Their mother had produced gems, Radhamohanbabu. With her blessings, all the children are well-settled. Wherever they were placed, there must they stay." He added a

Sanskrit shloka to that effect. "But the boys took turns to do the looking after. And over and above them all was my other sister by marriage, their aunt. She kept her elder brother confined within the shelter of her arms, and never let the children feel the absence of their mother. I was quite a regular visitor, you see. The pan was ready in time, so were the fruit juice, tea, sherbet, sweetened bel fruit, flea-seed husks; all set to a rhythm from which there was no departure."

"Really! Is that so?" The mobile mouth of Das Sahib became more agitated. "Rakhaharibabu must have indeed been a man of great virtue. As for me, having married off my only daughter in Canada, I keep counting my days, so that I don't have to suffer the loss of my wife. It's my prayer night and day. You know how it is—even a dog would shed tears for a widower. So where is this pious sister of ours? Let us bless our eyes with a glimpse of her!"

Both Atish and Anish realized that Das Sahib had become somewhat senile. But recalling that this tiger sans claws and teeth was once a man of immense power and a guardian angel to this family, Anish said, "Rontu, go and fetch Aunty."

Das Sahib had come on the day of the funeral ceremony, driving his old Morris Minor. But that day the brothers had been busy with the ceremony. All the elaborate rites were performed exactly according to the scriptures. The priest, a university professor, wouldn't tolerate any compromise. Consequently there was little time for social intercourse. Having listened to the devotional songs, rewarded the singers, sat at the ceremony for ten minutes, and had his share of sweets and a cold drink, the old man had departed along with the rest of them.

Atish was getting into quite a state bringing Aunty out of the ladies sitting room upstairs, down the steps, and across the big veranda. If only Das Sahib had asked for his wife Shukla instead, it would have been a more pleasing and easier chore. Shukla is sociable, witty, and pleasant looking. Not just pleasant, she is downright beautiful. After twelve days of mourning, she was looking gorgeous in her golden silk Tangail sari, her nails painted, her hair shampooed, and vermilion on her forehead. She would have come smartly, talked sweetly. But escorting Aunty was making him gasp for air. As it is she was over seventy-three. In a stiffly starched, plain white sari which her nieces and the wives of her nephews had made her wear, she looked just like a pod that had outgrown the fruit. With her rheumatic legs, she suddenly looked eighty, now that her brother was dead. Helpless, immobile, like a bundle. With eyes that didn't see, feet that couldn't move. Annoyed, Atish said, "Do you have legs made of straw, Aunty? And who put you in these stylish clothes? It's standing up around you like Queen Elizabeth's gown! God help me!"

Other than a few missing molars, at her age Aunty still had most of her teeth. She said, "I can do so little nowadays, my child, my sweet. Now all of you are my eyes, my legs. If you can take me along, well and good. If not, I'll just sit down here."

Atish said, "Help! Why did you have to stop? Don't you know, Das Sahib wants to meet you?"

The last batch to be fed had only the members of the family and the helpers. Seeing that Aunty was still willing to wait, Anish's wife Pratima insisted, "That can't be, Aunty. You must go and lie down now."

Aunty said, "You come from East Bengal, darling; how can you possibly talk of lying down in the afternoon? I don't need to rest."

"You haven't even eaten anything."

"What? Two fat bananas, a fistful of wet flattened rice, sweets! Enough to drown in. I've crossed seventy-three—in my seventy-fourth year—just a bit once a day and my body carries on as usual. I last out on the strength of my mind, not of my body any longer, my sweets."

Pulling a low stool toward her, she settled down on one side.

"Have a little of the smoked fish, darlings, Shukla, Mejobouma, don't throw it away. Just swallow it with the rice, as you would the banana on Dashara.*"

Anish remarked, "These old customs are not there any more, Aunty. Forget about them."

Shukla asked Atish, "What is all this about swallowing bananas on the tenth day?"

"How do I know?" Atish replied.

Deepika was sitting on the other side. She said, "Why! Don't you remember, Mejda, Mother used to stuff a banana with bitter gourd and make us swallow it? Supposed to be a great antidote. It's true, we hardly ever fell ill. Twice a week the bitter chireta herb, twice a week the equally bitter kalmegh. Those were the days! Loud wails, thrashing limbs—what drama!"

By three in the afternoon the house was more or less empty. The relatives departed one by one. As it was a Sunday, all those invited had managed to come. They met each other after so long that much time was spent in get-

---

*Tenth day of the lunar fortnight of the second month of the Bengali calendar, Jaishtha. The date marks the descent of the river Ganga upon earth. On this day a bath in the Ganga relieves one of ten kinds of sin.

ting the latest news. The members of the older generation are all going—the lamps are going out one by one, they said as they left. The children of the family were either playing around with the furniture brought by the decorators, or falling off to sleep.

Anu came in to say, "I couldn't control your son, Didi. He has defeated me. Put away three-fourths of the chairs all by himself. The men from the decorators are sitting idle, smoking their bidis and grinding away. He has started on the tables now—those long wooden planks, that is."

Chewing a pan, Dipu asked in a lazy voice, "What are Dada and Mejda doing then?"

"You think they are anywhere around? Dada went to see off his father-in-law at the station. And Mejda too . . ."

Shukla said, "Hey, Mejdi! Watch out, I'm right here. Don't you say anything nasty about him!"

Anu turned to look at her. Itu was smiling. She said, "We three sisters say whatever we have to in public. We don't say it behind anyone's back, Mejoboudi."

Shukla laughed, "We had actually started on Bubulram."

Dipu said, "Oh yes, he is removing the furniture. Let him. It is better to start early with whatever one is going to do in later life."

"Is your son going to be a decorator or a caterer?" asked Anu.

"He'll be a Class IV government employee," replied Dipu. "What else can he be?"

Shukla commented, "How can you worry so much about a boy who comes first in class every time?"

Dipu said, "Do you think the Class IV employee has any less of an IQ? With the right guidance, some of them could have taken over from doctors and engineers. It is really a matter of inclination, Boudi. If someone is inclined toward cleaning up after other people, he will do just that in life. Aren't there other children here? Dada's Rai may have grown up. But what about your Kishen, or Anu's Sampi, Mampi? Are they picking up empty chairs, dirty tables, or dirty dishes?"

"Why leave out the activities of my son, Didi?" said Itu, "just see what he is rehearsing for the future."

Itu's son was only seven months old. He had just woken up from sleep, produced some waste matter, and was looking grumpy. Itu rolled with laughter, "Look at that! According to your formula, that's all my son's going to do all his life."

Dipu hit her sister playfully. Shukla had tears of laughter in her eyes. She said, "Really, Itu, you're the limit. Let's find out where your elder brothers and sisters have gone."

Itu shouted out to her, "Leave the others out of it. We all know who you're going to look for."

Everyone laughed. But after a while, Shukla actually appeared with four of them. Anu's husband hadn't managed to come today at all. Dipu's husband had attended the funeral ceremony and returned to Asansol. The only son-in-law present was the youngest—Itu's husband.

Atish folded the end of his dhoti and settled down in the middle of the group. "All right, say what you want to say to me," he said. "I hear everyone has been looking for me for a long time?"

Dipu said, "Actually it was only Shukla. But now that you are here, you may as well believe that it was all of us. It's really been a long time since the brothers and sisters got together. They say kings might meet often, but sisters never do. But in our case, we never even meet our brothers."

Anish asked, "Where are the children? I saw Dipu's son having a great argument with Ismail. Ismail claims that there is a doddering old man in his village who is 273 years old. Dipu's son says, that is impossible. He has read the name of a Chinese or a Russian in the Guinness Book of Records."

Anu said, "Really, it's so sad to be old, isn't it? How old was Father?"

"Eighty-three. He couldn't hear, couldn't see. No teeth to eat his favorite food with," replied Dipu.

Anish said, "But he had his dentures!"

Pratima said, "So what? Father wouldn't use them regularly. They used to hurt him a bit in the beginning as they usually do. My father had false teeth by the time he was in his sixties. But someone had gotten it into your father's head that dentures can cause cancer. So that was that."

"We'd been telling him to go through a cataract operation right from the time he was seventy," said Itu. "Mother was alive then and I wasn't married. All he said was he wasn't going to live for long and he could carry on with his eyes as they were till then."

Atish said, "From seventy, he reached eighty-three. Nowadays these operations are nothing at all; they let you go after two hours. If he had given me permission, I would have arranged for it. But he wouldn't allow it."

Dipu said, "It was only because of Aunty that he didn't become an invalid, didn't have bedsores. The two of them would shuffle up to the terrace together twice a day and look after the plants. Father went while he was still in reasonable shape. He didn't like to eat anything but vegetarian food lately."

Itu said, "But whenever we came, Aunty would get meat and fish."

Anu said, "Itu, do you remember Aunty's potato curry? And her fried notay leaves?"

"Of course I do!" replied Itu. "It's a funny story. I didn't used to have spinach and all those leaves. Didn't even like potatoes then. At my in-laws', in Bhagalpur, they have a Bihari Brahman. You can't imagine how bad his cooking is. He has no idea of Bengali food. My mother-in-law, being an advocate, doesn't pay any attention to the kitchen. I came back home after three months and peeped into Aunty's kitchen. Aunty said, 'Go and sit down, I'll get your lunch.' I said, 'Give me a little of whatever you have made yourself, Aunty.' Aunty said, 'You'll eat fried notay leaves?' 'Definitely.' Oh Didi, oh Boudi, you don't know how lovely it was! The taste lingered. In the evening she made soft, white parathas and potato curry. Not steamed potatoes. Just curry. But what a taste!"

Anu said, "She sends a basket full of homemade flour sweets every year to my in-laws' home. We have other sections of the family as our neighbors; we share the sweets with them. Now every year from the sixth day of the Durga Puja, they all come and ask me whether Aunty will send the sweets this year! Greedy pigs."

Atish said, "That's nothing. When I was first posted to Durgapur, I took Aunty there. She soon became a popular figure. My students and colleagues knew Aunty more than they knew me. In fact I was being introduced to people as 'Aunty's nephew'—all because of all those homemade sweets and pickles and what have you. In desperation I told her one day, 'Aunty, I brought you to solve my meal problems. And there you are, feeding all Durgapur. If you go on in this way, I'll soon be out on the street.' She laughed, 'Why, does someone want to have my cooking?' You know, P. R. Sen was an absolute glutton. He was badgering me. Aunty said soothingly, 'Let me see what I can do.' That evening, when P. R. Sen arrived, she offered him a plate of her sweets and said, 'Pinaki dear, I've been wanting to do something with your help.' P. R. Sen said, 'This nephew is always at your command. Just tell me how many times I'll have to go to the market.' Aunty replied, 'Well, yes, dear, that's just it. I very much want to feed your family at your home.' Put him on the spot. But he loved Aunty so much, he just picked her up in his arms and danced around the room. I didn't have to do a thing. He arranged for Aunty to feed all our colleagues on the campus. The applause was deafening."

Dipu said, "Aunty must be very clever. I'm sure an IQ test will place her above the average."

"Very possible," said Atish. "Even Mother had a terrific memory. She could recall the year and the day of any incident. When Itu had said something funny, where Rontu had picked up his Asiatic cholera, what I had been discussing with my friends—Mother could repeat everything exactly. What an intellect. A lot of our old people in this country are like that. They all retain their original brainpower. But where is Aunty now?"

"Forced her to go and lie down a bit," said Anu and Itu.

Anish said, "There is something important to discuss. We may as well get it over with now. It would have been better if the brothers-in-law had been present as well. As they are not here, we'll have to sort this out among ourselves."

Anu was slightly apprehensive at Anish's tone of voice. "Why are you so serious, Dada? Say whatever you want to say with a smile. The way you're going on, it's giving me palpitations."

Anish lowered his voice, "In this huge house, Aunty will be alone now. Have you thought of that? Totally alone. Is it right to allow an old woman of seventy-three to live this way?"

"That's true! What do we do? There's not even a reliable servant in the house," said Dipu.

Atish said, "Forget it. You can't leave such a large house and an old woman in the hands of any servant, reliable or no. The only solution is for one of us to be here. Anu, you could do that!"

Anu or Anita lived in Ballygunj Place, her husband had his own firm of auditors somewhere near Garia. Her in-laws stayed with her. Anita said, "I could come and visit. But I can't live here. My father-in-law is seventy-four, my mother-in-law, sixty-nine. I have to look after them all the time. Sampi and Mampi are studying in Modern High. We had to make a lot of effort to get them admitted there."

Anish said, "Anu is the only one who lives in Calcutta. If she can't come and stay here, there is no question of the others. In that case the solution is to take Aunty with one of us. Just now everything is uncertain for me. Having been three years at one place I can get transferred anywhere any minute. Wherever it is, I'll get good enough accommodation all right. But I work in the danger zone. That's why I've sent Rai to a hostel. Even Pratima should not be with me. If I take a totally dependent old lady like Aunty with me, in a week's time Pratima or I will get a stroke just worrying. What do you say, Rontu?"

Atish said, "You know that I'm to leave for Germany in three months' time, Dada. I was planning to send Kishen to boarding school and take Shukla with me. Wives are allowed there. She won't get another chance such as this in her life. If I take Aunty, it won't be possible. Dipu, can't you? Anu and Itu both have their in-laws with them as well as other relatives. It wouldn't be right to take Aunty there."

Dipu hemmed and hawed, "He isn't here. I can't really decide anything without taking his opinion. Also, he is terribly bad tempered. I never hid that fact. All of you chose him for me, he is your brother-in-law. But when the man throws a tantrum at the drop of a hat, I can't take the risk of bringing Aunty into his home without asking his permission. And I know that he intensely dislikes having a third person in the house."

Anish sounded hopeless, "Then what?"

Atish said, "There's only one solution left. There are many good old people's homes available these days. Find a place for her in one of them."

Anish asked, "And the house?"

"Sell it and divide it among the five of us. Nobody will come to live in Srirampore. I've bought some land already in Durgapur. I can start building there if I get my share."

Anish looked thoughtful, "I, too, need a house. I'll probably settle in Delhi finally. The money would certainly come in handy. But there'll be little left after dividing it by five."

Dipu and Anu silently exchanged glances. Dipu said, "If it's a question of relinquishing our shares, your brothers-in-law should be present."

"Don't talk rubbish!" said Atish. "The shares will belong to you, not to our brothers-in-law. You can easily say whatever you want to yourselves."

Itu said, "We share a house with my in-laws; it's a large family. Whatever he earns, every paisa has to be handed to his father. Only I know what it is to have no money of one's own."

Anu said, "You're absolutely right. I, too, feel the same say. The keys are kept by the mother-in-law. The authority is hers and the labor is mine. If she ever gives any pocket money, you have to submit a debit-credit report, maintain a journal of accounts."

Dipu said, "You see, the house in Bhadreswar is their ancestral home, divided among seven brothers. You can imagine what it's like. Three of the brothers live elsewhere. The rest are all hanging on to the property. Whenever I've been back, I've stayed with Father. It will take us more than one lifetime to extract our share of my in-laws' property, buy some land, and build a house. If I get my share from this property, we could think of a roof over our heads somewhere, whether in Bhadreswar or in Asansol."

Anish said, "All right, all right. That's final then. Start looking for an old people's home. I'm here another week, we must make some arrangement within that time."

Just then there was a noise at the door. Aunty's close-cropped head became visible. She opened the door wide and said, "Dinu, my sweet, all my darlings are gathered here. Boro Bouma, my love, just pour out the tea for everyone from Dinu's tray, please."

Pratima and Itu both stood up. Pratima poured the tea and Itu passed on the cups. "What have you done, Aunty?" she exclaimed. "Fried fish, pompadoms, sweets! After that huge lunch?"

"Keep your mouth shut, silly girl," admonished Aunty. "You want to eat the tops of the puris alone and look like a rope to tie corpses with, that's up to you. Don't I know how many bites all of you took after feeding the guests to the gills in the afternoon? I didn't allow the cook to add all the fish to the gravy. Now go on eat, enjoy the hot food. Montu, don't you dare say no. Mejobouma, see that Rontu eats. He won't be able to say no to you. Dipu darling, I know you couldn't eat anything in the afternoon with that naughty son of yours around."

Anu said, "You didn't call me darling or love, Aunty. Didn't even ask me to eat. So I won't. There. Familiarity breeds contempt, doesn't it?"

Aunty's face broke into a wide grin, "I'll feed you myself, I'll place you on my knees, darling. You are very special. The Lord Shiva has daughters like Lakshmi and Saraswati. But his very own and dearest is Mother Manasa. She sits on the Lord's knees."

It is true that when Anu was born, her mother nearly died. For a long time she was not allowed to feed the baby, or even pick her up in her arms. Anu was brought up almost entirely by Aunty.

Shukla said, "Why don't you sit down, Aunty? Here, on this stool."

"Of course I will," said Aunty. "How can I resist being here, where all happiness has gathered? As God has still left me with my eyes, let me see all of you and fill my heart."

Atish said, "We have gathered here only to mark the end of the mourning for Father. And you call it a happy occasion, Aunty?"

"Why shouldn't I? Dada, too, must be saying the same thing up there—and laughing as he says it to Boudi. Unless we die, you don't come together, my loves. He has gone the best way. God willing, I too will go that way. And then all of you will gather like this, laugh and be happy, tease each other . . ."

Aunty wiped the tears from her eyes with the edge of her sari.

About three days later, after making inquiries, Atish came and told Anish, "Dada, there's a big problem."

"What is it?"

"The old people's homes are all right, but the better ones want large sums of money. Some of them even want it in advance."

"Did you check up with the missionary organizations?"

"I did, but you know what a strict Brahman she is. If we leave her in one of those places, Aunty might starve herself to death."

"Problematic." Anish looked thoughtful, "All right, let me tap the sources I have."

Finally, Anu's husband, Ranjit, brought news of a social service organization. It was run entirely by Hindus. But they looked after old people from all castes and creeds, free of cost. You could take a train there from Sealdah station. One day Anish and Atish went with Ranjit to check out the place. It seemed quite all right. They received secret donations from some big people, so they didn't charge anything. If anyone insisted, they might agree to a small donation. Next, the news had to be broken to Aunty.

Dipu said, "What will you do now, Aunty?"

"Do about what?"

"I mean, where will you live and how? Have you thought about that?"

Surprised, Aunty looked at all of them and said, "I have five children, not just one or two. At the age of seventy-three, do I have to worry about my own future?"

All the children remained silent. Ultimately, Atish said, "All right, we should do the worrying for you, then. You have given us permission to do so. Now listen. We have located a very good institution for you in Shyamnagar. You will stay there. They will look after you. We'll come and visit you whenever we can. It is an entirely Hindu setup. No Christians, no non-Hindus at all. You'll be able to live the way you want."

Aunty was staring in amazement. The end of her sari had fallen off her head in sheer surprise. Looking blankly at him she said, "Institution? What will an institution do for me, Rontu? Can't I stay here? In this Dash Gal?" The house was named Grace Dale. Aunty had always called it by a strange name, but that odd name had always remained her favorite.

Looking uncomfortable, Atish replied, "Of course you can stay here. But who will look after you? That's the problem. You're not getting any younger, are you? Is it easy to look after this huge house an keep it habitable? And where will we find such a reliable servant?"

"Why? Dinu will be here, Rontu. At the end of the month you can send a hundred or two, whatever you can, just as you did when your father was alive. It's been more than enough for me. You'll all visit me when you come this way. You'll stay, have your meals here."

"And what if you fall ill?"

"Nothing will happen to me, love. I'll go in my sleep. And Dinu is here."

"We can't trust or depend upon Dinu that much, Aunty. He will go to his village the moment it is harvest season. Won't turn up for two or three months. Ultimately the house will be taken over by squatters, you'll see. And that Dinu will help them to settle down."

"What will I do then?"

"You'll do what I said. You'll live in a beautiful place. When I come back from Germany, I'll take you with me. When Dada can, he will fetch you too. Just for now this seems to be the only possible way out."

Aunty said nothing. Anish and Atish had some work. They went out. The house agent was outside. Then they would have to go to the office of the municipality to find out what must be done about the mutation of the property. Everything had to be done in a short time. Pratima had gone to visit the neighbors with Rai. Rai had hair with a golden tinge, a fair complexion, and a face that was attractive if not beautiful. She studied in Miranda House. Seeing that little girl so grown up and so lovely at the funeral, the neighbors were all highly impressed. The social visits were a result of many invitations. Shukla sat for a while, then suddenly remembered that she hadn't seen Kishen in a while. Who knew what mischief he was up to with that naughty Bubul. She got up and left, calling for Kishen. Dipu was fiddling with her nails. The three sisters cautiously left Aunty's room one by one. Aunty went on sitting on the small stool. Evening fell on her face, then night. In just a few hours, Aunty became ten years older.

After all the papers were signed, Dipika said, "Could you tell us your visiting days and the hours, Mataji, we'll note them down."

Mataji lifted her head, "You're making a mistake. The people who come here have nobody in the world to call their own, nobody who can take their financial responsibility. So we don't have any visiting hours."

Taken aback, Anita asked, "No visiting hours?"

"No, we only keep those who have no one of their own." Anita recovered quickly, "That's true, of course. Aunty really has no one of her own. No children, no grandchildren, nobody."

Dipu said, "We are not her blood relations. Not her own family at all. Did you know that she was Father's stepsister?"

Itu said, "None of us knew that while Mother was alive."

"It was Mother's generosity. After all she came from a different family," added Anu.

Dipu said, "It was Father's generosity too."

This story would have ended here. That is the way it should have been. But it didn't happen like that. Late one night, Dipu started howling in her sleep. The noise woke up Asamanja, her bad-tempered husband. It woke her naughty son. Asamanja said, "What's the matter? Why are you raising the roof in the middle of the night?"

Dipu kept crying like a child, saying, "Tell me first whether you will allow me to keep Aunty with me, tell me! I'll be your slave for life. After Anu was born, I wouldn't eat anything unless she fed me with her own hands. I would place my hand on her breast, think her my mother, when I went to sleep. And that Aunty . . . Oh, I would have died without Aunty.

I had the rickets. You wouldn't have had me at all. Some other witch would have come to make your home."

Asamanja said, "Why start this in the middle of the night? You never told me you wanted to bring Aunty to stay with you?"

"How could I? You've such a temper! I wouldn't be as scared of Hitler as I am of you!"

"Then why blame me? It'll be wonderful if Aunty is here. She is a great cook. Go and fetch her. I won't have to suffer half-cooked food with too little salt and too much sugar. And this is what's making you cry?"

"What if your mother says something?"

"She'll only say it in Bhadreswar. Wouldn't reach our ears here. And if she does, she is my mother, I'll handle her. Oh! You women are so crafty."

"Not crafty, just cowards."

"All right, accepted. Now go to sleep."

Dipu came across Anu right at the station. All five of them now had a key to the collapsible inner gate of the Srirampore house. Dinu had the key to the outer door. Until the house was sold, he would stay as the caretaker.

Astonished, Anu said, "Didi?"

Dipu said, "Anu?"

Anu was looking tearful, "I dreamed last night of a thin, emaciated kitten whom Sampi was throwing across the wall. Suddenly the kitten cried out in a pathetic tone. And then I saw it was not a kitten at all, but Aunty! Didi, I can't leave Aunty in an old people's home. God will never forgive me then. When Mother was ill after giving birth to me, Aunty saved my life. It is she who is my real mother." Anu started weeping.

The two sisters shared a rickshaw and had a heart-to-heart on their way home. Dipu said, "I swear Anu, I've only been scared of my husband all this time. Terribly scared. If the socks aren't darned, he throws them away. If there's less salt in the dal, he throws that out, too. I had been summoned to Bubul's school and was late coming home. He just walked out of the house. God! That man! Today for the first time I respect him, perhaps love him too."

Anu said, "I thought a lot and decided that I'll come and stay here till the house gets sold. I've looked after my mother-in-law's son all this while. Let her look after my daughters for a change. Sampi and Mampi will come to this house Friday nights and go back with their father on Sundays. It's good for them to be a little self-reliant. Then when the house is sold, I'll take my share and keep Aunty as a paying guest in a South Indian home very near us. They would give a room, a bath, and a small kitchen, so she can cook for herself. Aunty will manage quite well, and I'll be able to look after her all the time."

The door of the house was opened by Atish himself. "What brings the two of you here?" he said in surprise.

"And what about you, Mejda?"

"Don't ask. Ever since we reached Durgapur, Shukla has been sulking. Yesterday she started making a terrible racket. Said, 'I won't go to Germany. If it is in my fate, I'll get another chance. If not, I don't care. I'm not greedy for anything foreign. You go. I'll stay here with Aunty and Kishen.' And then there was another incident."

"What incident?"

"Come inside. I'll show you."

On their way in, Atish shouted instructions to Dinu, "Make some good tea with soaked bay leaves. And start a curry or something. Two of the sisters are here."

Dinu came and said, "Give me some money, I'll go to the market. There's no kerosene either. I'll have to buy that too."

Suddenly the lights went off—load-shedding. The courtyard was covered with moss, the basil plant had become a little jungle. It wasn't looking like anything divine at all. More like a disheveled demon.

Atish said, "Be careful when you go to the bathroom, Dipu. The courtyard especially. I took such a toss . . . ugh!"

Dipu said, "We wouldn't have had to worry about such things if Aunty were here. The larder was always full, as if the generous goddess Annapurna had set up her store here. The house shone as if with the presence of Lakshmi herself. The courtyard slippery with moss, the house in darkness. Never in all my life have I seen it looking like this."

Atish scolded her, "Go on, do something about it quickly. Stop lecturing me. All your life, indeed! How long have you lived in this house? Five years or seven?"

Dinu said, "Whatever's five could be taken to be seven as well. Not much difference, Dababu."

When the electricity came back, Atish handed a telegram and an aerogram sent by fast mail to the sisters.

It was from Anish to Atish at Durgapur. "Am transferred to Delhi. Send Aunty sharp by the next Rajdhani. Awaiting information. Dada."

Itu's letter was also sent to Durgapur. She had written to both Atish and Shukla.

> Dear Mejda and Mejoboudi,
> Right from the beginning we did not like the idea of sending

Aunty to an old people's home. But I am after all the youngest, and also have a large household at my in-laws'. Your brother-in-law is not only shy, he is also the youngest in the family. For me it is unfortunately quite impossible to do anything about Aunty. But ever since I heard that they don't even allow anyone to visit her, I've been extremely unhappy. Discussing it at length with your brother-in-law, I discovered a legal point. Although Aunty was Father's stepsister, they shared the same father. And although Father had added to it a bit, Grace Dale in Srirampore was built by Grandfather. As such, Aunty should get a half share of the property. The other half we can divide up among ourselves. Aunty, therefore, is not as helpless as we believe. After selling the house, use her share of the money to put her in a really good place where we can go and visit her and bring her over when necessary. And if that is not possible, if you are going to deprive her after all, I would like to surrender my share. With that money, too, something similar could be arranged. Our ancestral property is built on about 700 square yards of land. One-fifth of that should be worth at least a lakh of rupees. With love.

Yours,
Itu

After reading the letter, Dipu said, "That's true, Mejda. According to the laws of today, Aunty should have a share in the property. None of us thought of that. Did you?"

Atish said, "Honestly, I didn't, Dipu."

They carried on their consultations late into the night. In the middle, Dinu went and got them some inedible roti and vegetable. There was no kerosene in the shops and Dinu didn't seem terribly keen on cooking for the four of them. Finally it was decided that they would fetch Aunty at once from Asha Niketan. The attempt to sell the house at Srirampore would be shelved for the moment. As long as Aunty was there, she should enjoy the house. Dinu would be there. If necessary, they'd look for another servant. Anu would supervise and come and spend the weekends here. Later, after Aunty's death, they could decide what was to be done with the house. Next morning, the three of them sent off telegrams to Anish and Itu, telling them about the new arrangements, and made their way toward Sealdah.

As the train moved, the three kept impatiently reading the name of each station.

Atish said, "You know, actually, for us, there has never been any difference between Aunty and our parents. Mother and Father looked at it that way."

Dipu said, "You've realized it a little late in the day, Mejda. In Aunty we had our father's blood and our mother's affection."

Anu said, "Do you remember how Mother used to call her Didimani? That tone of her voice? It was as if Mother and Father protected her with all their might because she was a child-widow."

Dipu said, "Last time I heard Father say, 'Ruchi, you must go before me,' Aunty said, 'Don't ever say such a thing, Dada. You go first. I'll come after you. Who'll look after you if I am not there?' 'And who'll look after you when I am gone?' asked Father. Aunty said, 'Don't worry about me. For a woman just a little bit goes a very long way.'"

The Mataji now in charge of Asha Niketan was not the one they had met earlier. Though it was difficult to tell at first sight. The same white clothes, the edge of the sari drawn behind the ears and round the head. She listened to them carefully and said, "You made a mistake, a terrible mistake. We don't take in anyone here who has any family. Society demands that people look after each other. Anyone who has someone to care for her wouldn't come to a charitable institution. It is the moral responsibility of her near and dear ones to look after her somehow. Why did you keep her here? Do you see the problem? We have branches of our institution all over India. We try to do whatever we can, not just for old people, but also for anybody who is alone and totally helpless. They all work for the institution as well. We don't keep the inmates too long in one place. Every few months they are taken to a new place. This is our rule. We never take any address for them. We don't even call them by their names. Besides a number, a new name is added for each member. We try to help them wipe out their past and build a new life here. As far as I remember, though, there haven't been any recent transfers. This name you gave me, Ruchishila Bhattacharya—I can't go inside and ask anyone about it. Here we are named after light, water, air, fire—Alo, Salil, Banhi, Varun, Pavan, Agun. I don't know who among them would be Ruchidevi, and cannot let you know either."

Seeing Anu in tears, Mataji relented, "All right. I'll do something for you. Stay in here; I'll darken the room. You see that square window—behind it is a veranda. I'll take the women inmates down the veranda. Keep count of them and tell me the number when you recognize her. After that I'll arrange to fetch her."

She shut the windows that looked outside, kept only the inner one open, and left the room.

A little while later the identity parade began outside the open window. The first woman had close-cropped hair, salt and pepper, a somewhat wrinkled face, not quite fair, not dark either. The second had shoulder-length hair, salt and pepper, a somewhat wrinkled face, not quite fair, not dark either. The third had close-cropped hair, all gray, a somewhat wrinkled face, not quite fair, not dark either. The procession ended after the thirteenth woman inmate. Mataji came in a little later, "Did you see them? Which one is she?"

Dipu said, "Who else? The first one."

"Never!" said Atish. "The third one. You didn't realize she has gone all gray."

Anu said, "I'm sure she's the fifth one."

Mataji said, "What? You say she is a close relative, your aunt, and you can't recognize her? All right, I'll go and ask these three ladies separately if one of them is Ruchishiladevi. Although, once again I must point out that this is against our rules."

Five minutes later Mataji returned to say, "None of them is called Ruchishila. The first one is Janakibai, a Bihari. The third one is Fatima Begum—obviously a Bengali Muslim. And the fifth one's name is just Butia. She used to live in a beggars' slum and never had a proper name. Even if she had one, she has forgotten it now. We call her Dharitri—earth. Why don't you do something—give us a recent photograph of your aunt, some identification mark, and a proper description. After that we'll see what can be done."

Then Atish, Dipu, and Anu talked it over at length among themselves and discovered that in the last ten years Aunty had never been photographed on any occasion. Also, that she was not too thin, nor fat; neither dark, nor fair; her hair was not all gray, nor all black; she hadn't lost all her teeth, nor did she have all of them; she was not too old, but certainly nothing less than old. Actually, she had no identifying mark on her. In fact, she was just an aunt. One of innumerable aunts. Not anyone's mother or father, just an aunt.

Translated from the original Bengali by Shampa Bannerjee

Glossary

bada sarkar	employer, usually the head of a feudal household
begum	upper-class, married woman, usually in feudal Muslim household
beta	son
bhain	sister
bharjaiji	sister-in-law
bijulee	local species of bamboo
bismillah	ceremony to mark a child's first reading of the Koran
bondas	appetizers stuffed with potatoes and fried in batter
brinjals	eggplant
chaddar	sheet
chal	makeshift housing, usually in Bombay slums
chanak chanak	sequins
chireta	bitter leaf used for medicinal purposes
chula	earthenware stove
chunni	long scarf worn across the shoulders or breasts (also called *dupatta*)

dharma	rule of the good
dholak	drum
diya	earthenware lamp
dupatta	long scarf worn across the shoulders or breasts (also called *chunni*)
durries	cloth rug
elaichi	cardamom
endi	thick, warm silk
gora paltan	foreigner
gulpashi	garland ceremony
haldi	turmeric
halechi, kollmu, nalakochu	local varieties of spinach in Assam
havan	ritual fire
jagir	piece of land given by rulers in earlier times as a reward for services
jajamans	Brahman family priests who earned a living by performing family rites
jamun	type of fruit
jatra	literally a journey; in this context, an event with songs, dance, drama, and stories
jora	suit of clothes
juba	long, gown-like garment
kajal	kohl
kalmegh	bitter leaf used for medicinal purposes
karhai	cooking vessel, shaped somewhat like a wok
khariya	type of fish
khes	woven cotton lining or covering for rope beds

kurta	long, loose shirt worn by men and women
Mahajan	moneylender
malida	cake made of pounded meal, milk, butter, and sugar
masi	mother's sister
mekhala	long skirt worn by Assamese women
mooras	cane and rope stools
mundu	piece of cloth worn around the waist by men and women in Kerala
munsif	title given to one connected with village administration
Murlidhar	Lord Krishna
nagalinga	canon ball tree
Namaz-e-Kaza	special Muslim prayer
nikah	Muslim marriage ceremony
notay	edible leaf
pakka	certain, confirmed
pallu	loose end of a sari, usually thrown over the shoulder
Panchayat	village council
parijat	white, perfumed flower; parijat trees shed flowers in the evenings
puja	prayer
punjabi	loose shirt worn by people from Punjab
sal	tree of the species Shorea
Satra	particular place
Sayyads	Muslim tribe which traces its descent from the Prophet Muhammad

satyagrahis	people who took part in Gandhi's satyagraha or noncooperation movement
Shandilya gotra	sub-caste among Brahmans
Shastras	holy books of the Hindus
shloka	holy couplets, usually chanted at ceremonies
sojji	sweet preparation made from cream of wheat
sraddha	death rituals
thali	plate, traditionally brass but more recently steel, out of which one eats
tol	traditional Sanskrit school
tongawalla	man who drives a horse-drawn carriage or tonga

Notes on Writers

MEENA ALEXANDER (b. 1951) spent her childhood in India and North Africa. She traveled to England for further studies and has taught at universities in India, the United States, and Canada. She is currently Professor of English and Creative Writing at Hunter College and the Graduate School and University Center, City University of New York. She is author of the memoir *Fault Lines* (The Feminist Press, 1992); the novel *Nampally Road*; and several volumes of poetry.

BANI BASU (b. 1939) was born in Calcutta and currently lives and works there. She is a novelist, poet, essayist, and short story writer. She has published three novels and several short stories in Bengali, and has translated stories by Somerset Maugham and D. H. Lawrence from English to Bengali.

AJEET COUR (b. 1934) was born in Lahore, Pakistan. She began writing at the age of sixteen, and by the time she was twenty-six had written over two hundred stories. A selection of twelve of these, *Gulbano*, was published in 1961 and won the Punjab Government Award in 1962. The first volume of her autobiography, *Khanabadosh*, won the Sahitya Akademi Award. She has published twelve volumes of stories and novellas, and one travelogue, *Kacche Rangan da Shehr*, which has been translated into Urdu and published in Pakistan.

INDIRA GOSWAMI (Mamoni Raisom Goswami, b. 1943) has published fifteen novels and three collections of short stories. In 1982 she was awarded the Sahitya Akademi Award for her novel *Mamare Dhara Tarowal* (Rusted Sword), and she won the Assam Sahitya Sabha Award for her novel *Unekh-*

jowa Howda (Moth-Eaten Saddle) in 1983. Her stories have been translated into various Indian languages, and she has published widely in research journals. Among her well-known published novels are *Chenabar Shrota, Neel Kanthi Braja*, and *Adha Lekha Dastave*. The recipient of many honors and citations, she was a member of the Advisory Committee of Sahitya Akademi, 1983–1988.

BINAPANI MOHANTY (b. 1936) started her literary career as a poet in 1955. She began writing short stories in 1956, and has published seventeen anthologies and two novels since then. She won the Orissa Sahitya Akademi Awards in 1971 and 1974 for her collection *Kastur Mruga O Sabuja Aranya*. Her story "Lata," which appears in this volume, was produced for television in 1986. She is the author of several one-act plays, her writing has appeared in the leading literary magazines of Orissa, and her work has been widely translated into many Indian languages.

DHIRUBEN PATEL (b. 1926), a prolific writer, is the author of twenty-seven books, three screenplays—among them the well-known *Bhavani Bhavai*—and six television serials, three each in Hindi and Gujarati. She is a recipient of the Ranjitram Suvarna Chandrak Award for her contribution to Gujarati literature, and was editor of a Gujarati weekly for nine years. She is a Professor of English in Bombay.

CHUDAMANI RAGHAVAN (b. 1931) was born in Madras and began writing in 1954. She has published thirty-two books and won the Tamil Nadu State Award for a novel in 1966. Her stories have been translated into various Indian languages and in 1962 she began writing in English as well.

K. SARASWATHI AMMA (1919–1966) was the youngest daughter of a Nair family in Trivandrum. She worked as a teacher and then as an accounts officer with the Kerala government. A prolific writer, she published twelve volumes containing over one hundred short stories, and was the first self-proclaimed feminist in Malayalam literature. Bold, outspoken, unconventional, and fiercely independent, she defied the conventions of a normal aristocratic upbringing and expressed without reserve her disapproval of male dominance over women. The last fifteen years of her life were spent in mysterious silence, with not a single line penned; she died, unsung and neglected, in 1966. Among her published works are *Premabhajanam* (novella), *Devadoothi* (play), *Shreejanmam* (short stories), *Purushanmarillatha Lokam* (essays).

RAJEE SETH (b. 1935) began writing in 1975. She has published one novel, *Tatsam*, which won the Bharatiya Bhasha Parishad and Hindi Academic Awards. She has published three collections of short stories and is coeditor of *Yugasakshi*, a Hindi journal. In 1985 she received the Katha Sahitya Ratna Puraskar Award.

WAJIDA TABASSUM (b. 1935) was born and raised in Amravati and Hyderabad, and is the author of twenty-seven books of fiction and poetry. Her story "Utran," which appears in this volume, was written in 1975 and has been translated into all major Indian languages. In 1988 it was made into a television program, and it has proved to be one of her most controversial stories. Widely traveled, Wajida Tabassum now lives and works in Bombay.